LOCK, STOCK, AND FERAL

COUNTRY COTTAGE MYSTERIES 15

ADDISON MOORE

BELLAMY BLOOM

Copyright © 2021 by Addison Moore, Bellamy Bloom
Edited by Paige Maroney Smith
Cover by Lou Harper, Cover Affairs
This novel is a work of fiction. Any resemblance to peoples either living or deceased is purely coincidental. Names, places, and characters are figments of the author's imagination. The author holds all rights to this work. It is illegal to reproduce this novel without written expressed consent from the author herself.
All Rights Reserved.
This eBook is for your personal enjoyment only. This eBook may not be re-sold or given away to other people. If you would like to share this eBook with another person, please purchase any additional copies for each reader. If you're reading this book and did not purchase it, or it was not purchased for your use only, then please return it and purchase your own copy. Thank you for respecting the hard work of this author.

Copyright © 2021 by Addison Moore, Bellamy Bloom

✾ Created with Vellum

BOOK DESCRIPTION

The Country Cottage Inn is known for its hospitality. Leaving can be murder.

My name is Bizzy Baker Wilder, and I can read minds. Not every mind, not every *time* but most of the time, and believe me when I say, it's not all it's cracked up to be.

A book club called the Grim Readers has descended on the inn and things take a turn for the deadly when life begins to imitate art. The weather isn't the only thing heating up in Cider Cove—tempers are flaring, too. Spring is in the air and so is murder.

Bizzy Baker Wilder runs the Country Cottage Inn, has the ability to pry into the darkest recesses of both the human and animal mind, and has just stumbled upon a body. With the help of her kitten, *Fish*, a mutt named Sherlock Bones, and an ornery yet dangerously good-looking homicide detective, Bizzy is determined to find the killer.

Cider Cove, Maine is the premier destination for fun and relaxation. But when a body turns up, it's the premier destination for murder.

CHAPTER 1

"A book club," I whisper in my sweet cat's ear as the makeshift library right here at the Country Cottage Inn begins to fill with bodies for tonight's literary shenanigans. "Finally something down-to-earth and grounded happening at the inn for once. I can't see a single thing going wrong tonight."

Fish, my sweet, black and white long-haired tabby, lets out a rawr. *You don't mean that, Bizzy.* She taps me on the chest with her paws as she does her best to stretch out in my arms. *You're on a murderous streak. I heard Jasper mention it this morning. Fourteen bodies in fourteen months. He says he may have overlooked a double homicide or two, but he wasn't caffeinated enough to do the murderous math.*

"Very funny."

She's right. My husband, Jasper, did say those exact words, and come to think of it, I'm pretty sure there was a double homicide in there somewhere, too.

My name is Bizzy Baker Wilder, and I can read minds—not every mind, not every time—but it happens, and believe me, it's not all it's cracked up to be—with the exception of conversations like these, of course. Yes, I can read the animal mind, too, and by and large, they have better things to say than most humans. I've got brown hair, blue eyes, and am average in just about every way with the exception of my aforementioned supernatural ability.

A body slams against my side as I narrowly move Fish out of the danger zone in time.

"Oh! I'm so sorry!" A heavy-set woman with long silver hair and pale blue eyes holds her hands spread wide before me as if she were about to steady me. She has on a denim dress and over her shoulder hangs a tote bag with cats embroidered all over it. "I've been in such a hurry to get here. I sped all the way to Cider Cove. I was afraid I'd miss the event altogether. My apologies again."

"No, it's okay," I say, rocking Fish. "We've got quite the crowd here tonight. I'm sure there will be a repeat performance soon enough as far as bumping into strangers goes. So where'd you come from?"

"I live in Rose Glen, so not far, but I was frazzled nonetheless." A soft smile comes to her face, and I can see that she has kind eyes, but overall she looks a little frayed around the edges. "I guess you could say I'm a little more than excited about tonight's selection."

"Oh? I take it you loved the book," I muse. "I just finished it last night, and I can't tell you how much I enjoyed it. What's not to love about a book that features both cats and murder?"

She sputters a small laugh. "Well, that's great that you got a kick out of it. I mean, cozy mysteries aren't for everybody. But they should be." She gives a tiny wink before heading straight for the wine station.

Yes, *wine*.

I scan the room and take in the heavenly scent of fresh brewed coffee. The library is more of a spacious sitting room with mahogany paneled walls and wooden floors stained a distressed shade of gray, both of which bleed into the rest of the inn as well. Shelves laden with books line the back of the room that acts as a lending library, and to the left sits a large stone fireplace that's already roaring with crackling flames. Rows and rows of folding chairs are set out in a circular pattern, along with a few wingback chairs and an overstuffed orange sofa near the back.

There's a refreshment table to my right with a coffee station, and I know for a fact a sweet treat is about to land right next to it. At the other end of the table, there's a spread of various cheeses, along with a bevy of wine to pair it with. It's not something I would have put out for an event like this—I'm more of a cookies and coffee girl myself—but the woman heading up the book club requested it.

I scan the crowd and my eyes snag on a man over by where the folding chairs are set out, who seems to be attracting more than his fair share of attention from the ladies.

Isn't he the cat's meow? Fish mewls with a note of sarcasm in her delivery.

"Seems to be," I whisper.

The man in question is tall, dark hair, blond at the tips. I'd say he has a decade on me, late thirties maybe. He's donned a fitted suit, a silver tie, and has that man-in-power feel about him, along with the fact he's textbook handsome, which explains why throngs of women are flocking to him by the minute.

He glances my way, and I quickly revert my attention back to the refreshment table where Jordy, the handyman here at the inn, hoists a wine bottle my way as if he were toasting me and I give a wave back with one of Fish's paws.

I asked Jordy to play the part of the bartender for the evening. Fun fact: Jordy is my ex-husband of one day. Vegas and bad whiskey were involved. Thankfully, my brother had just graduated law school, within his specialty of family law, and he took on my divorce pro bono. Nonetheless, I didn't want the guests tonight to have to serve themselves the liquor and God forbid a minor get schnockered on my watch. I made sure Jordy would be carding the guests, too.

Sitting in the middle of the refreshment table is a large purple easel that reads *Welcome to the Grim Readers Book Club! Tonight's selection is* Lock, Stock, and Double Barrel Peril! *Come for the book. Stay for the murder.*

A shiver runs through me as I read that last sentence, but before I can process it an all too familiar brunette steps in front of me with a conniving smile curving her lips.

Fish lets out a loud yowl at the sight of her. **Wicked witch alert! Run, Bizzy, run!** she teases. Or at least I think she's teasing. Come to think of it, most likely not.

"Camila," I say with a note of surprise and Fish recoils at the sight of her.

Camila Ryder was once my husband's fiancée. Now she simply stalks him while parading around as his secretary down at the sheriff's department. But lately she's donned the hat, or the crown as it were, as the gossip queen of Maine. Camila started a YouTube channel last month called *Gossip Gal* where she slaps on makeup while noshing on pizza and gabbing about all the local dirt she can dish in an hour.

She's tall, gorgeous, and her chestnut hair has a life of its own. She's stuffed herself into a light blue dress that clings to her every curve, and in her arms she's cradling a copy of tonight's book club selection.

Next to her stands a redhead in jeans and a T-shirt, holding a copy of tonight's book, too. She has big brown eyes, glossy red lips, and a face that could easily grace a magazine cover or two.

"Well, if it isn't our resident amateur sleuth." Camila gives a sly wink my way. "I've got a mystery for you, Bizzy." She hitches her head back at the redhead. "Meet my friend, Hadley Culpepper. Does the name ring a bell?"

My mouth opens as I look to the woman, and she offers a timid yet toothy smile my way.

"I'm sorry, have we met?" I ask as I search her features for answers. She looks vaguely familiar, but I can't quite pinpoint why.

"I don't think so," she says. "And don't worry. I'm just as confused. Camila has been teasing me, too." *For as much fun as Camila can be, she can be that much of a drama queen. Some things never change.* "She's just been terrible tonight."

Fish mewls, *So she's saying Camila is simply being herself.*

"That's enough for now." Camila takes the woman by the hand. "We'll talk soon enough, Bizzy." *And that will be a conversation you will never forget.* She waves with her book as they saunter over to the wine station.

"She's terrible, all right," I whisper to Fish.

When Jasper and I started dating, Camila tried her hardest to get him back, but all of her attempts failed miserably—thankfully for me. She could have landed Jasper the first time around, but she decided to cheat on him with his best friend, Leo. And, well, that ended badly for everyone involved.

Fish yowls. ***Would you look at Sherlock?*** she hisses as her tail whips toward the refreshment table. ***He's whimpering like a common beggar. Can't you control that mutt? Besides, he shouldn't be snacking. He's looking a little portly around the edges. It's time to cut back on the bacon if you ask me.***

Sure enough, Sherlock Bones sits like the rather *committed* beggar he is, looking up at all of the bodies gathered around the refreshment table with those big brown eyes of his. Sherlock was Jasper's dog before we were married, and now he's most certainly mine. I love both Fish and Sherlock as if they were my children.

Sherlock is a medium-sized mixed breed that sort of looks like a red and white freckled version of a German shepherd. He's as adorable as he is smart, and he's far too cunning when it comes to securing a cache of bacon for himself. He can't help it. Salted meat is his kryptonite.

I'm about to comment on his portly state when Devan Abner, the woman putting on tonight's book club meeting, heads my way.

"Bizzy!" she trills my name with a gleam in her bright amber eyes. Devan is tall, blonde, plain but friendly features, dressed conservatively with corduroys and a floral blouse buttoned to her neck. She had stopped by the inn a couple times to discuss tonight's gathering of her book club—and to request the wine and cheese. She offered to cover all costs, so I didn't say no. And she agreed to have Jordy supervise the liquor, which made me feel better about the whole thing.

"Everything is going so great." She gives Fish a quick pat on the forehead. "I'm so glad you suggested opening it up to the community. Who knows? The Grim Readers might just score a few more members yet."

"The book was adorable," I tell her. "I have no doubt people will be happy to join."

Her attention is momentarily diverted to that swarm of women all clamoring to speak to the handsome man in the suit.

And there he is. She snarls his way. *He thinks he's got it all together. Life is just so great for him, isn't it? He wouldn't be anywhere if it weren't for me. And tonight, I'll make sure he never forgets it.*

"Devan?" I lean her way. "Who is that man in the suit that these women can't seem to get enough of? It's almost as if a star were in our midst the way they're going at it."

She snorts out a laugh. "That's Patterson Higgins."

"Patterson Higgins? That's quite a name."

"Well, some say he's quite a guy." Any trace of a smile falls from her face, her eyes still very much pinned on his. I'm guessing she's not one of the people who thinks that way. "We'll start in a few minutes."

She takes off toward the refreshment table, and I watch as she makes a beeline for the wine. I'm sensing a theme tonight.

Fish mewls, *Oh, she's got the hots for him, too, Bizzy. I could see it in her eyes.*

"I bet you're right."

Speaking of eyes, that man in the suit looks my way again, and if I'm not mistaken, it looks as if he's edging his way in this direction.

Murder is afoot, a somewhat androgynous voice erupts from the crowd, and it's muted enough for me to tell it was a passing thought by someone in the crowd, and now I'm left to wonder if they're right. Unless a person is standing in front of me, it can get tricky to delineate if it came from a man or a woman.

Murder is afoot?

My internal radar goes off.

I can't help it. After finding so many bodies in such a small spate of time, an actual murder seems rather plausible—almost inevitable at this point. But then again, tonight's book club selection revolves around a murder, so I'm sure it was nothing more than someone reflecting on the book at hand. Or at least, that's what I'm hoping.

"Bizzy!" a female voice shrills from behind and I turn to find my sister, Macy Baker, older by one year, feistier by a millennium. Her short blonde hair curves around her jawline and her bright blue eyes are wide with terror. "Take it"—she thrusts something orange and furry my way and a few seconds tick by before it registers she's just handed me a small orange tabby with eyes the color of an unblemished afternoon sky. "You know I can't stand pets unless they belong to someone else."

Fish brays out a laugh as she taps her paw over the tiny kitten's head. **It's true. Macy is hardly a people person, let** *alone a pet person. But don't worry. Bizzy more than makes up for it.*

The kitten mewls and shakes but doesn't say a word in response.

I don't say a word either because my sister isn't in the know when it comes to my supernatural quirk. Only a small handful of people know I have the ability to pry into their gray matter, and I plan on keeping the exclusive club, *exclusive*.

The handsome man in the suit pops up next to us and Macy's mouth falls open because, let's be honest, he's that much more handsome up close.

"What a cute little kitten," he says as he gives a quick scratch between the tiny thing's ears. "I was just coming over to say hi to this one." He sheds an affable smile in Fish's direction.

Macy gags on a laugh. "How about that?" She bats her lashes at him as she scoops the orange tabby right back out of my hand. "No one is a bigger fan of cats than I am," she says, threading her arm through his and leading him off to the slaughter. Not only is she a brazen liar when the occasion calls for it, but she has an insatiable appetite when it comes to handsome men.

The warm scent of an all too familiar spiced cologne engulfs me from behind just before a set of strong arms wraps themselves around my body.

"Rumor has it a gorgeous innkeeper loves to duck out of these kinds of events to head up a fun club of her own."

A dark gurgle of a laugh strums through me as I spin in

my handsome husband's arms. Jasper and I met over a year ago while he was working on a case concerning that first body I stumbled upon. He's the lead homicide detective down in Seaview County, and he's been my lead man ever since the day we met.

"The rumors are true," I say, looking up into his lightning gray eyes. Jasper is handsome to a fault. Dark hair, dark smattering of stubble on his cheeks, and a dangerous smile that's known to crest on his lips make me swoon anew each time I see him. "But the club is strictly for two. Play your cards right and I'll indoctrinate you as a full-fledged member a little later."

No sooner do his lips twitch than Camila Ryder zips up with the pretty redhead dutifully by her side once again.

It's showtime, Bizzy! "Hello, Jasper." Camila gives an open-mouthed smile up at her ex-fiancé. "Guess who's here for the book club tonight? I believe you once referred to her as *the one that got away*? It's Hadley Culpepper!"

My mouth falls open as Jasper and Hadley exchange dumbfounded stares.

"The one who got away?" I meant for it to come out playful, almost teasing, but it came out with just as much shock as I'm currently feeling.

"Hadley?" Jasper's arms glide off of me as he takes a step in her direction.

"Jasper Wilder." A smile cinches on the redhead's face. *And to think I let this one go all because I was afraid.* "Come here, you handsome beast." She wraps her arms around him and they exchange a rather spirited embrace.

You handsome beast? Fish muses. ***Why do I get the feeling this woman is trouble?***

I make a face in their direction.

As much as I hate to admit it, Fish just might be right.

Camila chortles to herself as she joins the happy couple.

Murder is afoot tonight.

And I might just be the one to do it.

CHAPTER 2

I*'m sorry, Bizzy,** Jasper says as he glances my way. ***Do you mind if I take a minute?

I wave him off as if to say, *Take all the time you need. With the one that got away, no less.* I can't help but wrinkle my nose at the woman when that last thought flies through my mind, but Jasper is already too immersed in their conversation to notice.

Of course, my husband knows I can read minds.

And speaking of another person who's well aware of my telepathic prowling abilities, Georgie Conner, an eighty-something woman with long, gray, scraggly hair (think electrocuted by way of a socket), and sparkling blue eyes barrels this way with my mother on her heels. Georgie has a penchant for wearing nothing but comfy kaftans. The kaftan in question tonight is lavender, and it just so happens to bring out the mischief in Georgie's eyes. Georgie is a diehard hippie who happens to be an artist who specializes in mosaics.

"Well, if it isn't my favorite two old broads," I say a touch too loud as I force a smile. A part of me is hoping Jasper's old flame will see that I'm not threatened in the least by her redheaded, pouty-lipped, hourglass-figured presence.

I'm not, am I?

Regardless, *the two old broads* sentiment wasn't a putdown for two of my favorite women. Mom and Georgie happen to own a shop down on Main Street that sells everything from quilts to mosaics with the same zany moniker, Two Old Broads. My sister thought of the name, and to everyone's surprise, the general public loves it.

"You won't believe it, Bizzy," Georgie says as she wags the book of the hour at me.

"You liked the book?" I ask.

"Eh." She shrugs.

Mom balks her way. "What do you mean, eh? The book was really good. It was a *killer* read." She chuckles my way.

Mom is petite with dainty features, wears her hair feathered back circa 1980-something, and her wardrobe more or less pays homage to that very same totally rad era as well, as evidenced by tonight's floral popped collar blouse and tapered jeans.

Georgie growls as she takes Fish from me. Georgie just so happens to be one of the brave and the few who are in on my telesensual secret—that's the proper name for my gift. Telesensual falls under the umbrella of transmundane, a broad spectrum of powers of which there are many.

"I didn't think much of the book." Georgie smacks Fish on the forehead with a kiss. "There was no action in it."

"No action?" Mom balks. "What about the big chase scene at the end with all the guns and the flying bullets?"

Georgie waves her off. "I meant action in the bedroom."

Mom rolls her eyes. "It's a cozy mystery, Georgie. They're not exactly known for their torrid love scenes."

"Why not?" Georgie is quick to question the lust levels of an entire genre of mysteries.

"I don't know," Mom shrills with just as much fervor. "Maybe the people who write them hate sex."

Georgie chokes on her next breath. "Hate sex? How do they think they got here?"

"All right, ladies." I give a loose smile at the handful of heads that have turned our way. "Let's keep it G. This is a family show tonight, despite the wine."

"You've got wine?" Mom's eyes spring wide open at the prospect of vino. "This just gets better and better." She giggles, and I inch back a notch.

"Did you just giggle?" I ask.

Fish yowls, ***Ree Baker does not giggle. Perhaps she's already hit the vino?***

Perhaps so.

Georgie smacks my mother on the arm. "Go on, Toots, and spill the French beans or I'll be forced to do it myself."

"What French beans?" My antennae go up without hesitation.

"Fine." Mom is back to glowering at the ceiling a moment. "I met a man." She shrugs. "You and your siblings are forever after me to get out there and meet someone, and so I've taken your advice."

I choose to momentarily overlook the fact I've never said such a thing.

"Where did you meet this person? Please tell me it's not some stalker you picked up from that YouTube show you're running?" For the last few weeks, Georgie and my mother have been hosting a half hour show out of their shop as a way to drum up some business. They're just showcasing new products more or less, and telling odd jokes—and I do mean odd—and they've done a recipe or two. They don't have an explosive audience, but they think they do. And they're convinced it's boosted business by twenty percent—whatever that means.

Mom shakes her head. "No, he's not a stalker. He's a businessman. His name is Romero. He's from Wichita, but he's currently in Paris scouting a European location to expand his business."

"Romero from Wichita," I say. "What kind of business?" I ask, cocking my head with suspicion.

"Software something or other. We're still getting to know one another, so I'm not prying too deep. We met on that app that's all the rage for people over fifty, Dating Not Waiting. It's completely safe, so you don't have to worry about me."

Georgie's phone chirps and she all but tosses Fish in the air as she yanks it out of her pocket.

"Ah-ha!" She fiddles with the screen a moment. "I've got another one!"

"Another what?" my mother asks and I'm glad she did because I was almost afraid to go there.

Georgie makes a face her way. "You're not the only one with another shtick going. I've got me another gig, too. I signed onto Rent-a-Grandma. This is my second booking this week. The first one was some old kook who wanted to watch Fun Flix and chill."

I gasp at the thought. "Georgie! That man was a pervert."

"Well, for a pervert, he sure missed his mark. After one solid minute, he fell asleep. The movie wasn't so bad, though."

A cool breeze whistles our way just as my best friend, Emmie, waltzes in along with her fiancé, Leo Granger, and they each just so happen to be holding a platter of—green cookies?

"Why are they green?" Mom makes a face, but Georgie

takes one for the team and shoves a green disc into her mouth.

"Because they're delicious!" Georgie moans as she scoops up a few more for herself.

"Thank you," Emmie says. "They're pistachio pudding delights. Although they do sort of look like green chocolate chip cookies, I can assure you they can hold their own in the yummy department."

Both Emmie and I share the same long dark hair, denim blue eyes, and we even share the same formal moniker—Elizabeth. But since we've been friends forever, we've both gone by the nicknames our families have gifted us—Emmie and Bizzy.

"Take one, Biz." Emmie stops shy of shoving her platter my way. "Hey? Who's that woman Jasper is arguing with?"

"Arguing?" I quickly turn in his direction, and sure enough, Jasper and Hadley have drifted a bit and seem to be going at it while Camila snickers on the sidelines. And just past them, the woman who bumped into me earlier in the evening with the long silver hair seems to be having a heated conversation with Patterson, the looker, along with another gentleman, a lanky man in a maroon sweater.

Odd. The hostile nature of their conversation almost acts as an echo to the one Jasper seems to be having.

What in the world could have Jasper in such a rage?

A hard groan comes from Leo. ***Oh no. Not her.***

I gasp as I turn to Leo. "What do you mean *not her*?"

Leo Granger is the one person I know who actually shares my mindreading abilities. He's telesensual as well.

He happens to be engaged to Emmie, and because of this, Emmie is apprised of our well-guarded secret. Leo is Jasper's best friend—the very best friend that Camila cheated on Jasper with. That pretty much put a damper on Leo and Jasper's friendship until about a year ago when they made up. But now things are great between them, and not only do they work together at the Seaview Sheriff's Department where Leo is a deputy, but they're paired up with a couple of lifelong besties.

"Never mind, Bizzy," Leo mutters as he takes off in their direction, and before I can follow, Devan Abner gives a sharp whistle and asks that everyone take their seats.

Every person in the room scrambles to do just that, and I end up with Jasper on one side of me and Georgie on the other.

Sherlock trots over and settles on the floor between Jasper and me. *Don't tell Emmie, but I don't think her cookies look very delicious. She should try adding some bacon to them next time.*

Fish hisses in his direction, *Humans don't like bacon in their cookies, you ninny.*

Surprisingly, sometimes they do.

Macy tiptoes this way and bumps Jasper over a seat, promptly taking his place.

"Here, take this," she whispers, shoving the tiny orange ball of fluff my way. "If anyone asks, his name is Clyde and I adopted him from a nearby shelter last week."

"And where did Clyde really come from?" I ask. The last time we were about to get to that part of the conversation, Patterson Higgins and his well-fitted suit interrupted.

"I found him cowering behind a pot outside of the inn."

"Aww," I coo at the sweet thing. "He must be a stray."

What's a stray? the tiny cutie mewls while shivering with fear in my arms, and judging by the higher pitch to its inner voice, I'm betting Clyde is a girl. Our inner voices almost always mimic what our vocal cords produce.

Apparently, you are, Fish mewls right back.

I don't know how the animals seem to understand one another, but they always do.

This is Bizzy, the one holding you, Fish yowls her way. ***And she can hear your thoughts and understand you. Once we're away from the other bipeds, she'll be happy to speak with you further. For now, you'll have to wait until we're through here. They'll be discussing a murder. And if I'm right, we'll be treated to one as well. Bizzy is delinquent one, rather*** **hostile,** ***homicide. It's sort of a hobby of hers to stumble upon the dead.***

A body hunter! Clyde twitches her whiskers my way as if the thought delighted her.

My mouth falls open as I give both of the cats a look. I shake my head, trying to brush the thought of a murder out of my mind for now.

I pick the tiny orange thing up and do a quick inspection, and sure enough, I'm right.

"He's a *she*," I say to my sister. "And I can take her from here."

"No way," Macy whispers through the side of her

mouth. "As soon as we're ready to mingle again, Clyde is mine. She's my ticket to the inner workings of Patterson Higgins' darkest chambers—i.e., his bedroom." A dark laugh strums through her just as Devan Abner stands at the front of our circle.

"Welcome everyone to the Grim Readers Book Club!" Devan calls out, and her blonde mane glistens under the lights as she garners the attention of everyone in the room. "On behalf of the original members, I want to welcome all of the new faces we have here tonight. And I want to thank Bizzy Baker Wilder, the owner of the Country Cottage Inn, for graciously hosting us here tonight. The wine, the cheese, the cookies are all fantastic!"

A light applause erupts in agreement.

It's true, I do own the inn. I inherited it just last December after the original owner met a rather untimely demise. I still get shivers thinking about the poor man's murder. As much as I hate to admit it, Fish is right. According to the homicidal pattern we seem to be in, we're due for yet another untimely demise.

Devan holds up the book in her hand. The cover has a picture of a lavender field with a bright blue sky and a discarded revolver.

"Tonight's selection is *Lock, Stock, and Double Barrel Peril* by S.L. Teller," she raises her voice as she says it. "Who here has finished the book?"

Almost every hand in the room goes up save for Macy, but once Patterson Higgins glances in this direction, her hand shoots up like a bottle rocket.

"Okay!" Devan does her best to sound like an enthusiastic book coach ready to cheer us to the literary finish line. "Let's open up the floor with what you liked best about the book. Anyone like to go first?"

"The cover," someone shouts from the back and the room fills with groans and chuckles.

Georgie scoffs. "That's because it needed a little hanky-panky in it."

Patterson gives a pained smile as he raises his hand. "In the author's defense, the novel was centered around a murder investigation. It's tough to work a little romance in there. Does anyone want to give a brief synopsis of the book to get us going?"

That's interesting. I guess he's a moderator, too. He must be one of the lead members.

"How about you, Hadley?" His lips curve in the redhead's direction, but she's not smiling back. In fact, she looks as if she's shooting daggers at him.

Macy gasps as she leans my way. "I knew that was her. That's Hadley Culpepper."

I inch back and examine my sister. "How in the world do you know her?" I leave out the detail of her being the one that got away from my husband.

"You know her, too," she whispers. "We used to watch her on that show, *Esmeralda the Teenage Magician*. I think it was the only thing she did in Hollywood. I read an article a few years back that said she got out of the business—it wasn't for her or something like that."

Georgie leans in. "That's what they all say when they can't get work."

Oh my stars, I do remember that show! I was completely addicted. Esmeralda was my very last Halloween costume as a teenager. I used to wish Emmie and I could meet her so that the three of us could be best friends. And to think she'd go on to sleep with my own husband one day.

I sit up straight as I look over at Jasper.

Did she sleep with my husband?

Jasper glances my way and does a double take.

Everything okay? His brows furrow as he asks the question.

No. Everything is not okay.

I turn to face the front again. I'll deal with him later.

Hadley clears her throat, her eyes still sharpened over Patterson's. "Why, I *would* like to give a synopsis. It was a typical pig in a poke plotline. The main character, Summerset, was tricked into purchasing a worthless gold mine. Jed, the murder victim, sprayed down a stretch of land with gold dust and requested a mint for it—which Summerset happily paid after he begged, borrowed, and stole from his parents. Once he realized he'd been had, he tried to demand his money back. And when that didn't work, he decided to kill Jed."

"Good." Patterson winks her way. "You have quite the way with words, Ms. Culpepper. That was a perfect synopsis." **And later tonight I'll give her a perfect synopsis of how I feel about her—with my body.**

My mouth falls open at hearing the salacious thought. I won't lie. It thrills me to know she has another romantic prospect on the horizon who is not my husband. In fact, Patterson can take a bottle of wine with him on the way out. Heck, they can *both* take a bottle. I might take one myself and make a party out of it with Jasper. Only I won't be mentioning a thing about Hadley and her perfect toothy grin to him.

I can't believe he slept with *Esmeralda*. Worse yet, I can't believe I'm steaming mad over it. I'm being ridiculous and I can't seem to control it. The next thing you know, I'll fall into a jealous rage and start throwing books at her.

Devan lifts her chin. "Anybody like to fill the rest of the room in on how Summerset murdered Jed?"

"Shelly?" Patterson nods to the woman with the long gray hair, the heavier woman who I bumped into earlier this evening.

"It's Liv," she corrects him, and that snippy tone in her voice doesn't go unnoticed. *I bet they would like me to review it.* "It would be my pleasure."

She glowers over in their direction, but I can't tell if she's upset with Devan or with Patterson. I'm going to go out on a limb and say it's the handsome man in the suit. I get the feeling the only people who can tolerate him are the hordes of women who are after him—like my sister. And I bet not one of them is interested in his personality.

Liv glances down at the book in her hand. "Summerset killed Jed by injecting bitter orange into his wine. A toxic compound he cooked down to ensure the maximum deadly benefits."

"That's right," Devan says. "But Summerset's problems with Jed didn't end there, did they? What happened to Summerset after Jed died?"

Mom raises her hand, and a tiny spear of pride infiltrates me. My mother always has something intelligent to say.

"Go on." Devan nods her way.

"Summerset fell in love with Lydia, his next-door neighbor."

The room breaks out into titters, and even Devan herself laughs the idea off.

"Well, I think that's a bit of a stretch, don't you think?" Devan tips an ear toward my mother. "I mean, at most they had a few exchanges about how their chickens were doing and whose poultry was producing more eggs."

"Oh, but those conversations were so very sensual." Mom swoons, and another round of cackles circles the room once again.

So much for having anything intellectual to say. That French-American she's quasi-dating has turned her brain to mush.

The tiny kitten in my hand mewls, and I draw her closer to me.

Even Clyde can see that my mother has her head in the clouds. Thankfully, Romero—if that's his real name—is too far away for her to have any of her other body parts mixed up in the endeavor.

"Anybody else?" Devan scans the room for a moment until her gaze stops cold over Patterson.

"I'll give it a go." He winks her way, and it only seems to infuriate her all the more.

"Go on." *All right, hot shot, let's hear how your genius mind will interpret this disaster. I'm betting you'll be twice as randy as Drooling Debbie over there.*

Did she just call my mother Drooling Debbie? She's not far off the mark, but for my mother's sake, I'd like to request a less bodily fluid based moniker. Like maybe Delusional Debbie or Desperate Debbie.

Patterson gurgles a quiet laugh. "I think Summerset is a good example of many of us. We fight for something we believe in. We discard the old, and pound our chest that we're free of it, so much so that we start to buy the lie that it was holding us back all along. But in truth, life is never that cut and dry. Many things can hold us back. Often, we like to finger point and suggest it was one thing, one person. But as it turns out, many times it was us all along. We dole out the power for people and things to hold us back. And with Summerset, even long after Jed was gone, I think he realized he was still in that emotional cage. Jed might have been dead, but Summerset was far from free of him. Summerset blamed Jed for his own ruin. He put him on a toxic emotional pedestal. Some people are simply tethered together so tightly it's impossible to ever be free of them."

Devan's head tips to the side as if he struck her. "So you think Summerset had the power to free himself, and yet you said that he was still in an emotional cage? What stopped Summerset from letting go of his emotional baggage and finally breaking free?"

Patterson bores his gaze right into Devan's. "Summerset will always care about Jed."

The room breaks out with a nervous laugh, and Devan fans herself with her book.

"It seems Mr. Higgins read the same copy as our chicken friend here," she says while throwing daggers his way.

A warm laugh circles the room on my mother's behalf and she joins in blushing like a schoolgirl.

Devan leads the room into another discussion before she announces a five-minute coffee break, and soon the room is alive with conversation once again.

Jasper heads my way. "I see you have a new buddy," he says, giving Clyde a quick scratch between the ears. "You'll like Bizzy. She's extra friendly to cute kiddos like you."

"Apparently, you're extra friendly, too," the words speed out of me a touch too quickly, and it's no use, I can't hide my irrational jealously. Jasper is just going to have to take my budding rage on the chin like a man.

A dry laugh pumps from him, but he's not smiling. "Did you pick up anything? You know, from her mind?"

"No." I make a face. "At least not about you."

He glances back into the crowd. "I'll be right back, Bizzy." He drops a kiss to my forehead before speeding off.

Perfect. He's probably going to warn her that his wife is

a weirdo who reads minds, and that she should keep their budding romance on the down low.

I crane my neck into the sea of people and spot Emmie and Leo trying to shill their green cookies. Jordy is pouring wine as fast as he can, and I see Devan and Liv, the woman I bumped into, as takers. Next to Liv is that man in the sweater I saw earlier. He looks pretty eager to get in on the liquor action himself. And low and behold, stepping up to the front of the line are Jasper and his new hottie, Hadley Culpepper.

I can't help but shake my head when Jordy all but bows to the woman and hands her the very next glass of wine. I bet that's exactly how Hadley has gone through life, cutting lines and stealing husbands. She's a magician, all right. She's doing pretty well at making my husband disappear.

I spot Devan in the corner with that man, Patterson, and they look as if they're having one heck of a tense conversation. I doubt it has anything to do with the book. I sensed something wasn't right between the two of them during our little meet-up.

A few dizzying minutes go by and I spot Sherlock by the door that leads into the main hall, so I head on over and nearly bump the wine right out of the hands of the lanky man in the sweater.

"I'm so sorry," I say as I move past him.

Bizzy! I found the killer! Sherlock Bones gives a few quick barks, but the noise level is so high in the room it sounded more like a whisper.

"There's not a real killer. It's just a book we're

discussing," I say, bending over and giving him a quick pat. "This is Clyde." I hold out the fluffy tangerine in my arms. "She's new here. I'm sure we'll get to know all about her as soon as we get back to the cottage."

Clyde lets out a tiny whimper of a mewl. *Oh, I like you. What's your name, big boy?*

A laugh gets caught in my throat as I pull her back to get a better look at her.

"That's Sherlock Bones. He's as friendly as can be. And if you keep batting your lashes at him, he'll hand over all his bacon to you. He'll deny it all day long, but he has a soft spot for cute kittens. Just ask Fish."

I do not! Sherlock is quick to bark. *I hardly like Fish at all.* His left ear hikes up a notch as if to contest his words.

Well, I hope he likes me, she purrs. *I know I like what I see.*

I'm about to lower her so the two of them can get to know one another a little better when the sound of agitated voices streams from the other side of the door.

I take a quick peek outside, and just as quickly step next to the door as not to be seen. It's Patterson and Hadley, and they look as if they're having a heated conversation.

"I can't keep doing this with you," she hisses. "And to be honest, I have better prospects on the horizon. If you don't make something come of this quickly, I'm walking."

I bet Jasper is that better prospect.

"If you want this to work, then I'll need a little more," he says, swallowing down the last word, and I can't quite make it out. He'll need a little more what? Time beneath the sheets? *Money?*

"I've given you more than I care to admit," she seethes. "I'm walking."

"You can't walk. I *own* you."

Silence ensues.

I bet she's shooting daggers at him, just the way she was inside.

Hadley flies past me, followed by Patterson who strolls on in before stopping right next to me. A touch of surprise takes over his face as he spots me.

"Cheers," he says, toasting me with his wine before knocking back his drink. "Here's to all the beautiful women." He winks as he walks deeper into the room. The man in the sweater walks up to him, and he seems to be telling Patterson something urgent.

Before too long, Devan calls the room to order, and we all take our seats once again.

"Okay, class." Devan laughs as she says it. "Who here is ready for the grand finale? A foray into *murder.*"

Patterson spikes out of his seat and a croaking noise escapes him. His face is a bright shade of red, then purple. He grips his left arm, then staggers into the center of our circle.

"All right." Devan gives a slow clap. "You win the prize for most dramatic reenactment. Now do us all a favor and die already." She shoots Hadley a knowing look. "Some of us here would love to savor the moment."

Patterson does his best to point a finger in her direction, but he doesn't hold it up for a solid second before he collapses in a heap at her feet.

The room grows quiet before the woman with the long silver hair breaks out into an applause, and the rest of the room follows suit. But Patterson doesn't so much as twitch a muscle in response.

Jasper hops out of his chair. "I don't think he's faking."

Both he and Leo dart over to the man and quickly check his vitals.

Jasper shakes his head over at me.

Patterson won't have to worry about beautiful women anymore.

Patterson Higgins is dead.

CHAPTER 3

"He's dead?" Devan jumps to her feet and knocks the chair out from behind her.

Georgie hops right out of her seat, too. "It was the green cookies!" she shouts and tosses Fish into the air by proxy.

Fish, my highly talented cat, doesn't merely land on the

floor, she somehow swims through the air and lands right onto the back of the man who just bit the big one.

The entire room lets out a horrific groan before a series of screams and sobs break out among us.

"Georgie." I shake my head at her. "There is nothing wrong with those cookies." I hope. "You're going to land the health inspector at the inn."

"You're going to land the coroner at the inn—but then, you always do."

"I can't argue with that." I sigh.

This isn't our first rodeo with a body dropping to the floor.

"Give me the kitten, Bizzy." She thrusts her gnarled fingers my way and I quickly move Clyde out of her grasp.

"Why?" I ask. "So you can throw her at the poor man, too?"

Clyde hisses in Georgie's direction—as she should. Cats are smart in general, but Clyde seems to be especially intuitive. Speaking of cats, I spot Fish all but riding on Sherlock's back like the Queen of the Nile, right next to Patterson's body, and horror upon horror, people are snapping pictures of the adorable yet macabre sight.

What is happening?

Macy steps our way and clucks her tongue. "Maybe if you threw more kittens at corpses they'd stop happening." She shoves her fists into her hips. "Way to go, Bizzy. You offed another one. And to think you didn't have the decency to wait until after I was through with him."

I can't help but scoff at my ridiculous sister just as both the fire department and the sheriff's department swarm the room.

Mom steps up and wraps an arm around Macy.

"There, there." Mom tries her best to comfort her older daughter. "How about I help you set up a profile on Dating Not Waiting?"

Macy squints over at the woman who bore her. "That meet-your-geezer match place?"

"That's right." Mom pats Macy on the arm. "I think an older man will do you some good. They're settled, financially stable, and experienced."

"What kind of experience?" Macy muses, suddenly interested in broadening her geezer horizons as they walk off into the crowd—and I'm thankful for it, too. That's one conversation I didn't need to hear the conclusion to.

Georgie makes a play for Clyde, but the tiny tot uses my chest as a springboard and does an acrobatic leap through the air, cartwheeling twice before landing rather heroically onto Sherlock's back as well, and the crowd around us breaks out into a spontaneous applause.

"Oh my word." I cringe at the sight.

Clyde all but hugs Sherlock's bottom with all four of her limbs while Fish spins around and swipes at the tiny tot with her tail.

You saved me, Clyde mewls as she gives Sherlock a quick lick.

More like he got in the way, Fish corrects. *Come with me, we'll head over to the cottage until this all blows over.*

I'm not going anywhere without this big, strong, handsome hunk to protect me. The tiny kitten looks as if she's digging her claws into Sherlock's hind end.

Fish's whiskers twitch as she looks around. *What handsome hunk?*

Sherlock barks and offers that perennial smile he's known for as he looks my way. *I think she's talking about me, Fish. I'm the handsome hunk!* He does an awkward sidestep to his left and accidentally steps on Patterson's head. *GAH! Dead guy! I stepped on the dead guy!*

Sherlock's body jerks and inadvertently launches both cats onto Patterson Higgins' aforementioned dead body and causes the fur on them to rise to the ceiling. Both Fish and Clyde let out hair-raising yowls before bolting right out of the library, and I'm guessing right out of the inn altogether.

"Sherlock," I whisper. "Please make sure Clyde doesn't run away. I don't want her out there all by herself."

Fish most likely won't care one way or another. She understands that cats can fend for themselves. And truth be told, I think her radar is up with that little orange kitten, seeing that Clyde is ready to pounce on her man.

Leo jogs over. "What's with the flying cats?"

"Sorry. It was an odd sight, I know." I crane my neck into the crowd until I come upon another odd sight. "What's with the irate ex-girlfriend?" I ask, nodding over to where Jasper and Hadley look as if they're having another heated conversation.

"Oh that." He grimaces. "Why don't you take care of the inn? I'll escort Hadley out of here."

"Are you hauling her down to the station?" The words come out with a touch too much glee. I can't help it. I think every woman who makes a play for my man deserves to be behind bars. Not that she made a blatant play for him, but I'm getting bad vibes—and if I've grown to trust anything, it's my vibes.

Leo chuckles. "I don't think she's making a play for him."

I frown over at Leo. It's easy for me to forget he can pry into my gray matter.

"I'm sending her home." He nods back her way. "I need to free up Jasper so he can get to work."

"Leo, you can't send her home. She's a suspect. And the *prime* suspect in my book. I heard her arguing with the victim. I don't think she should be getting preferential treatment just because she's *the one that got away*."

"Whoa. You're going dark." A stunted laugh comes from him. "Emmie," he calls out as he flags down his other half. "Why don't you help Bizzy in getting some semblance of order around here?"

"Leo, you're changing the subject." My words come out curt. "I'm not letting you play into the fact she's Jasper's ex. I think someone should talk to her—obviously not Jasper. He's far too close to the situation."

Leo squelches a smile. "Look, we have no proof this was a homicide. The guy may have had a run-of-the-mill heart attack for all we know. Let's everybody calm down."

"I'm not calming down," I say, taking a step in his direction. "And Jasper certainly doesn't seem to be calming down either." I glance his way just in time to see Jasper looking right at me, and if I'm not mistaken, he's visibly upset.

Jasper turns back to the woman before him and says something to her before taking off for the cluster of sheriff's deputies.

Hadley casts a glance my way. The hardness in her eyes assures me we won't be friends anytime soon. She nods a moment as if agreeing with the fact before stalking over to the lanky man in the sweater.

"Him too," I say to Leo. "I saw that man that Hadley is speaking with arguing with the deceased as well. They're both suspects."

"All right," he says, nodding to Emmie. "Let's get Bizzy out of here. I'm sure if this turns into a homicide investigation, you'll be the first to know. You're married to the lead homicide detective." He pats me on the back. "Don't worry about Hadley. She's old news." He takes off and I shake my head in his wake.

"Old news?" I shoot Emmie a look. "She's brand new to me. And judging by Jasper's reaction to the woman, they seem to have a bit of unfinished business."

"Leo is right. She's his past, you're his future. You're not an insecure person, Bizzy. You're just tired, and this entire fiasco isn't helping. In fact, what can *I* do to help?"

"Head to the front desk and see if they need anything. I'll make sure things wrap up in here."

Emmie makes a face. "I see what you're doing. And because I'm loyal, I'll do what you want, but if I were you, I'd steer clear of that Hadley person until you've had a chance to talk to Jasper about it."

She takes off and I scan the room as bodies buzz back and forth. A majority of the crowd is huddled toward the back, and that's exactly where I see Devan Abner talking to the most handsome man in the room, the one who just so happened to land me in a vat full of unexpected jealousy—my husband.

Emmie is right. I'm exhausted. This entire event has been taxing from the get-go.

I'm being silly. Jasper and I are fine.

I thread my way over to where they're standing and shed a pained smile to the blonde before us.

"I'm sorry about your friend," I tell her.

"Oh, he wasn't my friend." Devan's eyes grow in size a moment as if to annunciate her point. She nods up at Jasper. "If you need me at all, you have my number. Excuse me, I see a few of the regular members by the door and I'd like to speak to them before they leave." She takes off and it's just Jasper and me.

The air between us feels slightly strained, and I shake my head because I'm positive it's all in my mind.

"Everything okay?" I ask with caution.

Jasper's gray eyes widen a moment as he looks deep into mine, and try as I might to read his thoughts, they're not coming through. All I'm getting is strangled buzz, not the kind of white noise that I pick up on when someone is having naughty thoughts. I've always considered that a sort of override system that spares me from accidentally prying into anything too graphic, but this—this feels very much purposeful on his part—almost as if he's struggling to hide his thoughts from me.

"I'm sorry, Bizzy." He pulls me close and lands a kiss over the top of my head. "I promise, I'll tell you everything, but this isn't the time or place." He hitches his head toward the body on the floor. "I'd better get moving just in case this turns out to be something nefarious."

"Sure," I say, but he's already gone.

Something nefarious is going on, all right.

I glance back to where Hadley and the lanky man in the sweater stand, and they've been joined with Devan as the three of them sneak glances to where Patterson Higgins lies lifeless. Just past them is that woman with the long silver hair, Liv, standing with her lips knotted up as she observes the scene as well.

Someone is going to have to pay for this. And it won't be me.

A voice spouts off, and yet I can't be sure who said it.

Pay for this? That's a curious thought.

My feet carry me in Liv's direction as I step up beside her, joining her as we watch the sheriff's department swarm around a man who seemed perfectly healthy less than twenty minutes ago.

"What do you think happened?" I ask without breaking my gaze from the chaos before us.

"Oh, I think we both know what happened," she says,

nodding to the trio to our right. "Someone finally offed the poor man."

"What do you mean *finally*?" I ask.

Her pale eyes glow against her tawny skin and her hair looks as if it's lit from the inside as well. She almost doesn't look real. In fact, nothing about this night *feels* real.

"You know." She gives a casual shrug. "Patterson had a few friends, but he had far more enemies. Then again, rumors of a heart attack are swirling."

"I've heard the same. You don't believe them, do you?"

She shakes her head. "Perhaps I would have if it were anyone else. Not for him, though. Never him." She cinches her tote bag over her shoulder. "I guess he won't be at the next meeting." She takes off for the refreshment table, and I'm left stunned in the wake of her callous words.

On second thought, I can't judge her. I can't judge anyone's thoughts or words at a time like this. Everyone is in shock. Nobody is themselves when faced with a body in the room, whether a natural death occurred or foul play was involved.

I take a few steps over to Hadley, Devan, and the lanky man ensconced between them.

Is it possible to hate someone twice as much for dying? one of them says, and I take another step closer.

I give it twenty-four hours before news of his demise spreads. We all knew this was coming.

It's finally happened. Patterson Higgins gets his just desserts, and I get to witness it firsthand. Life couldn't be better. Death couldn't be sweeter.

It wasn't some run-of-the-mill heart attack that did him in.

It was murder.

CHAPTER 4

"Blueberry pancakes, lobster roll, lobster pie, clam chowder, crispy clams, clambake weekends. And for dessert, I say we focus on several flavors of whoopie pies," Emmie says as we stand on the sprawling patio just outside the Country Cottage Café. Fish and Sherlock are taking Clyde for an afternoon run up and down the sandy cove, and they have about twelve different children running along after them.

It's April, spring is here, the air is warm, and the cove is brimming with tourists in bathing suits as the scent of fresh grilled burgers competes with coconut-scented suntan lotion.

Emmie heads up the café for me, and since I firmly hold the reins to the inn now, we've decided to make a few changes, one of which is a total revamp of the menu. Not only that, but I splurged for an entire outdoor grilling area that was recently installed as a way to feed those guests who are far too sandy and wet to venture into the café.

The Country Cottage Inn is a tall, stately building constructed primarily of blue cobblestones, much like the ones that snake around all of the arteries leading to and from the inn. Although it's hard to tell what color the inn is considering it's nearly camouflaged in ivy. The property is set on a vast acreage, and there are more than thirty cottages we rent out. Jasper and I happen to live in one, Emmie lives in another, and Georgie lives in one as well.

There's a pet daycare center in the back of the inn that caters to both the guests and the townspeople of Cider Cove called Critter Corner. I had come up with the idea because I didn't have the heart to turn away guests with pets. And thanks to my love for all things furry, the inn has been voted the most pet friendly resort along the coast of Maine.

The inn butts up against a sandy cove that stretches out in either direction. But the real star of the show is the gorgeous Atlantic Ocean, with its powerful navy waves and the never-ending spectacle of whitewash slapping against the shore.

"Yes to all of it," I say to Emmie as we go over the prospective menu options we're thinking about implementing. "What about crab cakes?"

"I knew I was forgetting something. Of course, we're serving crab cakes." She quickly jots it down. "And you're okay with lobster in its every iteration?"

"I'm more than okay with it. Maine catches ninety percent of the country's lobster. We practically owe it to our guests to serve it in its every iteration. And as soon as you whip up a lobster pie, I want the very first bite." I wrinkle my nose at the row of thatched umbrellas dotting the sand and the rows and rows of blue and white striped lounge chairs set out for the guests to enjoy. "Although, my appetite is waning."

"You're still hung up on that Hadley woman, aren't you?"

"Do you realize she played Esmeralda in *Esmeralda the Teenage Magician*? She's a star, and she's beautiful, and—she and Jasper spent all night arguing about who knows what."

She winces. "Leo filled me in. He said Hadley and Jasper were pretty serious for almost a year, but that it ended abruptly. I guess that was before Camila. I'm sorry, Bizzy. I can imagine Camila's glee when she told you about that whole *one that got away thing*. So what did Jasper have to say for himself?"

"Nothing yet. He came home at three-thirty in the

morning and was out the door before I got up. He said we'd catch up on everything tonight."

Fish, Clyde, and Sherlock scamper in this direction as both Fish and Clyde jump right into my arms before a gaggle of kids can snatch them. But Sherlock isn't that lucky, he's mobbed in an instant.

"I got this," Emmie says. "Hey kids?" she shouts. "Who would like some free cookies?"

The crowd of pint-sized hellions screams with delight as they follow her to the café.

"That was a close one," I say, giving both Fish and Clyde a kiss in turn.

Last night when we got back to the cottage, Clyde told us all about the fact she was born in a field nearby and that she and her siblings all had to fend for themselves. Considering the fact she's not at all scrawny, I'd say she was excellent at keeping her tummy full. But regardless, she has an appointment with the vet in an hour, and I'm making sure she keeps it. But I haven't said a peep about it to the furry among us. No sooner do I say the V word than both Fish and Sherlock start shivering like a leaf—not to mention they go into hiding and make it impossible to catch them.

Clyde mewls up at me and her eyes shine like cobalt. *The little one with pigtails wanted to take me home!* she snips it out rather incensed.

"That's because you're so cute."

Fish lets out a hearty meow. *It's because she's playful. I'm sorry to tell you, Bizzy, but she clawed her way up the curtains this morning before you woke up. I tried to stop her.*

I suck in a quick breath. "You don't want to do that, Clyde. You could fall and hurt yourself."

Fish yowls, *What Bizzy is trying to say is you could hurt her curtains. The curtains are off-limits, as are the countertops and the table. And don't even think of using the furniture as a scratching post or she'll pull out the clippers and cut your claws off.*

Clyde hops right out of my arms and lands on Sherlock's back with a plop. *I won't touch anything of yours, Bizzy, if you promise not to get near my claws. I need them to survive. Besides*—she wraps her limbs over Sherlock's back as if she were holding on for dear life. *Mr. Bones here will protect me. Won't you, sugar?* She gives his fur a few quick licks. *A big, strong animal like you could protect just about anybody.*

Sherlock makes an odd yelping noise in response. *I'm especially protective of cute little kittens such as yourself.*

Oh brother. Fish rolls her eyes.

Come on—Clyde spurs him on with a pat of her paws—*take me for a ride. Why don't you show me around this place, big boy?*

Fish ticks her head back and scoffs as the two of them lumber on down the cobblestone walk. *Would you look at that?* She turns her head my way with a jerk. *She's shamelessly flirting with him so he'll do her bidding. You saw it yourself. Clyde is outright using him.*

"I wouldn't say that she's using him. I think she genuinely likes him. Besides, Sherlock is perfectly loveable. We can't blame her for falling head over paws. He's a cutie."

He's an oaf.

A tiny laugh tickles my chest. "Yes, but he's *your* oaf."

Fish moans. *You're right. We need to send that kitten back into the fields. She's disrupting the natural order of things.*

"Bizzy!" a female voice shrills, and I turn to find Georgie and her sixty-something-year-old daughter Juniper Moonbeam, aka Juni, running down the walkway.

"Speaking of disturbing the natural order of things," I say as I wave back. "How's it going, ladies?"

Georgie has on a powder pink kaftan, and Juni is wearing a denim mini skirt with a lime green tank top and slung over her shoulder is a quilted tote bag.

Juni was once my stepmother for all of five minutes, or so it seemed. My father is sort of a bride magnet and she was number three or thirteen, I lost count. I like to tease that I got Georgie in the divorce. Juni looks exactly like Georgie but with less gray hair and a few less crow's feet. But she has the same wily gleam in her eyes and same wily disposition.

"What's cookin', good lookin'?" Georgie says as she gives my hair a quick tousle.

"You tell me," I say.

Two Old Broads only consists of Mom, Georgie, and Juni. And judging by the fact two of the three employees is here, it's safe to say they've left my mother to fend for herself.

"Let me guess," I say. "You're taking a lunch break?"

"You bet your little pink bottom," Georgie says as Sherlock and Clyde make a reappearance. "Give me this little girl. Come here, Clyde. Meet your Bonnie." She winks at the cute kitten as she excavates her from Sherlock's back.

"Juni, I love your quilted tote," I say, plucking at the cheery blue and pink floral fabric.

Two Old Broads is infamous for selling Georgie's wonky quilts in every configuration. Georgie came up with the wonky idea last October. A wonky quilt is essentially a quilt with large triangular shapes and frayed edges that can be whipped up quickly—and whipping them up quickly is exactly what they've been doing. They're not only selling them as traditional bed covering, they've turned these wonky quilts into tote bags, dresses, pet beds, pet blankets, curtains, and they're working on a bridal line, too. It's all been a rather natural progression. Considering the fact Georgie is an artist, none of this surprises me.

Right on their heels I spot my mother, giggling to herself while staring down at her phone. She's dressed in a cornflower blue sundress and has a striped wide-brimmed hat over her head to shelter her from the sun.

I squint over at her, trying to make sense of this. "Considering the fact all three employees of Two Old Broads are front and center, I take it you closed down the shop for the day?"

"What?" Georgie spins and gags once she spots my mother. "Ree Baker! What are you doing? Who's manning the store?"

"What?" Mom practically tosses her phone in the sand as she comes to. "How did I get here?" She glances around in fright. "I heard someone say lunch break and I just grabbed my phone and started chatting with Romero. Oh, I'd better get back before we're robbed blind." She speeds off toward Main Street and Juni chuckles.

"That's a lady in love for ya," Juni says.

"In love?" I balk. "Please. My mother has had a hardened heart toward men ever since my father spurned her. She's not in love. She hardly believes in that four-letter word. Not romantically anyway."

"You're right," Georgie says while waving at me with Clyde's paw. "She believes in another four-letter word—*lust*. I saw the dude's picture. He could be a cover model on every planet in the solar system. He's got rock-hard abs and enough biceps to pick up all of Maine. Face it, your mother has a grade A beefcake on her hands."

Juni grunts, "No wonder she's losing her mind. The next thing you know, she'll be losing her knickers."

"Try grade A scammer," I say. "My mother had better not lose her knickers. I don't trust the guy."

Juni nods. "Guess who else you shouldn't trust?"

Georgie smacks her. "That was my line, kid." She leans my way. "Did you happen to catch that latest *Gossip Gal* episode this morning?"

"Don't tell me you actually watch Camila apply mascara while dishing on her so-called friends."

"We don't miss an episode," Juni is quick to confess. "And don't forget the yummy treats she eats while filming."

Georgie groans. "She inhaled a box of fresh glazed donuts right in front of us and she wasn't even sorry about it." She pats her stomach as if she were the one who inhaled them. "You should have seen it, Biz. She talked all about last night's book club bludgeoning."

"Nobody was bludgeoned," I say just below a whisper lest a guest or two pick up on the bloody conversation. It's bad enough my poor inn is amassing a reputation without Camila's help, but now that's she's pitching in, I have a feeling she's about to catapult us to an infamous status. Before I know it, all the inn will be good for is Halloween TV specials and homicide hungry lookie-loos.

"Eh." Juni shrugs. "I don't think she could find a word that played off of *book*, and *bludgeoning* sounded pretty good."

"Anyway"—Georgie tucks Clyde under her right armpit and it's a disconcerting sight—"she mentioned that a certain homicide detective from Seaview was reigniting a relationship with an old flame—one that happened to be a hot commodity in Hollywood not that long ago. Sorry to hear it, Biz. I take it Hux will be handling the divorce."

"What?" I squawk. "This is the first I'm hearing of a divorce."

"Who's getting a divorce?" a deep male voice calls from my left and I turn to see both my brother, Huxley, and his relatively new bride, Mackenzie Woods.

"Hey, Hux," I say as he gives me a quick hug and both Fish and Sherlock a quick scratch between the ears. "Hello, Mayor Woods." Even though Mackenzie has been my official sister-in-law for a couple of months now, I still prefer to call her by her formal and civic-minded moniker.

A million years ago Mackenzie and I used to be best friends right along with Emmie. But then she pushed me into a whiskey barrel full of water and held me under, thus sponsoring this mind-bending, mind-altering, mindreading ability of mine.

I may have had the telesensual tendencies in me since birth, but Mack's foray into attempted homicide sealed the deal. She also made quick work of giving me a few phobias that fated day as well—to both large bodies of water and confined spaces. Suffice it to say, I don't venture into that Atlantic bathtub very often beyond my big toe.

"How are you feeling?" I give Mackenzie the once-over. She's as gorgeous as she is blunt with her long dark hair, almond-shaped eyes, and perennial glowing tan. Although today she looks a little pasty, her hair is a bit mussed, and she's not wearing her typical power suit. Instead, she's donned a sage empire waist dress, which shows off the budding little pouch in which she's housing my niece or nephew. Mackenzie announced she was three months pregnant as soon as they came back from their shortened honeymoon. Their little bundle of joy—or if it takes after Mackenzie, bundle of terror—is due to arrive in September. And I can't wait to cuddle with it.

"I feel great," she says. "In fact, I'm here to have lunch with my handsome husband. Sorry to hear about the implosion of your marriage, Bizzy. I'm sure Hux will be happy to help you out—for half his typical fee."

"Half?" I stifle a laugh. "I'm sorry, but if I were to get a divorce, I'm sure my brother would help me out for free."

"Free?" She laughs at the thought. "Sorry to break it to you, Bizzy, but we're shopping for a house," she smarts. "And we have college tuition to think about now. I'd suggest if you want to save a dime, you might want to overlook your husband's philandering ways and give his mistress the boot."

A flood of words dams up in my throat and I choke on them.

"Jasper is not cheating on me." I shoot Georgie a look that phrases those exact words into a question. She's the one who doesn't miss an episode of Camila's *Gossip Gal* hour, not me.

Before Georgie can so much as give me a wink, Emmie appears in our midst holding out a platter of those fresh baked pistachio pudding wonders of hers.

"Cookies?" She extends the platter and Mackenzie groans at the sight of them.

"Why are they green?" Mackenzie no sooner gets the words out than she lets out an egregious belch. And in one quick move she plucks open Juni's wonky quilt tote and pukes in it.

"I guess she's not feeling so great after all," I say as I turn to Hux. "Just a heads-up, our mother might make *you* want to puke. She dove into the deep end of the cyber dating pool. You might want to check in on her now and again. She's acting erratically."

"Good to know," he says, patting Mackenzie on the back.

"Bathroom," Mackenzie says as she zips right past us and into the back of the inn.

"Wait!" Juni calls out, holding her bag out before her. "You forgot your breakfast!" She takes off after Mackenzie, and Hux gives a long blink my way.

"I'd better get in there," he says. "I knew she wasn't quite up for bopping around town, but Mack wanted to show the townspeople she's feeling fine."

My phone chirps and I pull it out. "It's a text from Jasper."

Georgie leans in. "What does it say?"

"It says he won't be home until late." My lips move feverishly as I quickly read every word. "Patterson Higgins didn't die of natural causes." I take a breath and hold it. "He was murdered."

"I could have told you that." Georgie swats me. "What do you think the killer dragged him to the inn for? This is the *it* place to knock off your enemies. I hope my enemies take note of it."

I shake my head down at my phone. "He says he needs to speak to Jordy since he was doling out the wine last night."

Hux clucks his tongue. "Sounds as if Jordy might need to lawyer up. I'll head in and touch base with him. And I'd better find my wife while I'm at it, or I'm the one that might be needing a divorce attorney. I'll see you ladies later. Stay out of trouble, Bizzy. Jasper was not giving you a license to investigate this case."

We watch as he disappears into the inn.

"The heck he wasn't," Georgie says, stealing Fish from my arms. "Now which one of you kitties is coming with us to track down a suspect?"

Sherlock barks. **What about me?**

Georgie rolls her eyes at the sweet cats. "Men. Can't live with 'em, can't enjoy bacon without them." She plucks a handful of salted meat from her pocket and tosses it his way. "So who are we drilling and grilling first, Bizzy? The butcher? The baker? The candlestick maker?"

"The one that got away."

Hadley Culpepper is the very first suspect on my list. I'm gunning for you, Hadley.

But the real question is, are you gunning for my husband?

CHAPTER 5

It turns out, Hadley Culpepper has chosen to eschew all social media.

I get it, she wants her privacy after living in the limelight for so many of her younger years—at least she said as much in an old interview I was able to dig up. But it's made tracking her down nearly impossible. After I drop Clyde off at the vet—and terrify Fish and Sherlock by proxy—I head back to the inn and decide to sort the mail until I can find a way to sink my claws into Hadley—just the way she managed to do my husband last night.

An entire thicket of people step into the foyer of the Country Cottage Inn and my trusty employees get straight to work checking them in while Sherlock gets straight to greeting them. Fish barely lifts an eyelid their way as she lazily whips her tail back and forth by my side.

I quickly scan the crowd in hopes by some miracle Hadley has wandered back to the scene of the crime—and by crime, I mean the attempted abduction of my husband —or at least his mind.

For the life of me I can't imagine what they were arguing about. In all the while I've known that man, I have never seen him that animated. He has never so much as raised a crooked eyebrow at me, let alone his voice. What if he's got some dark side that only Hadley is privy to? Would I really want to know about that?

My gut churns as I look to the faces of the guests at hand. Most of them are pink from too much sun, but not one of them belongs to her. My eyes snag on one face in particular, and I drop the mail I'm holding, scoop up Fish, and head toward the familiar woman with the long silver hair.

"Liv," I say a bit too cheery as if we were friends.

Easy, Bizzy, Fish says as she adjusts herself in my arms. *You keep squeezing me and I'll be the next one who needs to see the vet. And don't think I won't make my feelings clear on the matter if I get pricked and prodded. It's a torture chamber in there and we both know it. I may not care for Clyde's smitten disposition regarding Sherlock, but I wouldn't wish what that poor cat's going through on my worst enemy.*

All the way home from the vet's office I tried to explain to Fish and Sherlock why Clyde needed to be seen. But neither of them was buying that whole *it's for her own good* story. And they both demanded treats for the trauma I had imposed on them for bringing them along on the trip. Of course, I caved. Twice.

Liv turns my way and her mouth opens as she tries to process who I am.

"I'm Bizzy, the manager—owner actually of the inn. We met last night."

"Oh yes." She squeezes her eyes shut and laughs.

She's younger than her silver hair would let you believe, and a part of me wonders if she's dyed her tresses this color. It's stunning on her. I've seen people my age doing it. And honestly, it's only a few shades lighter than the platinum color Macy has been dying her locks.

"You were my hit-and-run of the night," she teases. "I didn't leave a bruise, did I?"

"No." I laugh. "I fared well. Can I help you with anything?"

"Oh yes." She gives Fish a quick scratch. "Actually, I came back for two reasons. One, because I just didn't feel like I had closure last night. I'm sure that sounds silly. But Patterson was a friend." Her eyes flit to the library. "And two"—it looks as if it takes herculean strength to pull her gaze back my way—"I have family coming from the West

Coast next month. I just visited them a few weeks ago in So Cal so it's tit for tat. And I can't house them at my place, so I thought I'd look into your rates while I was here."

"Well, for sure I can help you with that last part. In fact, I'll give you the friends and family discount, which is almost half off our summer fares. I feel just terrible about what happened. I'd invite you to go back into the library, but I'm afraid the sheriff's department still has it sealed off."

"Oh?" Her pale blue eyes widen a notch. "Why is that?"

"They suspect foul play. I don't have any details, but I guess anything could have happened to that man in there. I saw him getting worked up a few times. I mean, that alone could be foul play."

She nods. "You're right. It looked like a run-of-the-mill heart attack, but I guess you never know these days. It's as if the entire world has lost its mind." Her gaze drifts back toward the library with its doors sealed off like a tomb. *So much for saying goodbye, or good riddance. Thank goodness I didn't leave anything behind. I'd never get it back at this rate.*

I bite down on my lip. I can't judge her for a single thought. It wouldn't be fair.

"Hey, were you a regular member of the Grim Readers?" I ask. "I'm trying to hunt down one of its members."

"I sure am. Which one were you looking for?" *I bet it's Devan. Who else is there?*

"Hadley Culpepper." Her name stings a little as it leaves my lips.

Liv's forehead breaks out into a series of lines. "Oh yes,

Ms. Hoity-Toity." She averts her eyes. "She was the one everyone was always after—for her autograph. I never asked." She shakes her head as if it were silly.

To be honest, if it wasn't for her very intimate connection to my husband, I would have asked, too. And believe me, I'm angry with myself over this nonexistent event.

Liv tips her head back. "Where could she be? Oh, wait." She taps my hand with hers. "She was a part of some writers' group. I heard her mention it a time or two. We talked shop now and again. She's a budding author."

She's an author, too? Fish whips me with her tail. ***That's quite the competition, Bizzy.***

I frown down at my once sweet cat. It's clear she's going to make me pay for that trip to the vet in more ways than one.

"Liv, where do you think I can find this writers' group?"

"They meet at the Dream Bean out in Blueberry Grove, just south of Rose Glen."

"Nice," I say as I bounce on the balls of my feet, because obviously I can't wait to confront the hussy. "I haven't been to Blueberry Grove in some time. I'll head out that way and see if I can talk to her. Do you know when the club meets?"

"They meet each Thursday—so I guess that would be today." She glances down at her watch. "They started a half hour ago. You might want to hurry if you want to catch her."

"Wow, I will hurry. Let me get you a sheet with my rates, and don't forget you'll get the discount." I walk her back to the desk and hand her a pamphlet. "What week were you looking at?"

"We haven't settled it yet, but I think around Memorial Day."

"It's one of our busiest weekends. I'll jot your name down as tentative, that way you're certain to get a spot. Last name?"

"Womack." She winces. "That's my married name—or technically, it's my *divorced* name. I keep meaning to change it." ***I should have never taken his name, or come to think of it, his number.***

"I'm sorry about that."

"Hopefully, you'll never know that kind of pain. They say a divorce is like death, and they would be right. I was a homemaker for twenty years, and then poof, he left me to my own devices. Took off with his secretary and left me in the financial dust. I've recently blown through my retirement fund. It hasn't been easy. I was left to fend for myself while he continued to live the high life. Count your lucky stars you have this place. I'd better get going. I work down at the library, and I'm running late. I'll see you around, Bizzy. I'll let you know about booking the rooms as soon as I can." ***I might just stop by the cove now and again by myself. Lord knows I need the respite.***

"Thank you," I say as Sherlock heads this way.

Well, Bizzy? He gives a quick bark. ***Is she the killer?***

"No, but I have intel on where to find my prime suspect. Either of you up for visiting a coffee house?"

Sherlock growls, *Is that what they're calling the vet these days? No thanks. I'll take a nap until dinner.*

"Fish?"

I'll come under one condition, she mewls. *You don't even think of making a left on Main Street. Coffee house isn't code for torture chamber, is it?*

"No, but on the way home I need to pick up Clyde."

I'm staying in the car for that, she roars.

"Sounds good to me," I say.

And just like that, we're off to snag a cup of coffee and maybe a killer.

CHAPTER 6

The Dream Bean in Blueberry Grove holds the thick scent of coffee along with an under layer of perfume. It's homey with its fireplace raging in the corner and large tufted chairs set out here and there. It's laden with dark wooden chairs and matching floors, and there's even a bookcase that sits against the far wall to give this place a cozy appeal.

Throngs of women have infiltrated the place, most of which are situated with a laptop in front of them, along with notebooks, pens, and highlighters. The writers' group is made up of about a dozen or so women seated at a series of conjoined tables near the back, each of them already sipping on the coffee and noshing on a sweet treat. A friendly looking blonde goes from one woman to the next, observing their work and giving feedback, and I bet that's the ring leader here. But it's not her I'm here to question.

I spot the exact redhead I'm hoping to nab, seated on the end with a few free seats next to her.

"Oh, there she is," I hiss at Georgie and my mother. Once Juni heard there might be a writing assignment involved, she volunteered to hold the fort down at Two Old Broads, but my mother and Georgie jumped at the chance to tag along. "Let's hurry and get our coffee. Remember, let me do all the talking."

Fish pokes her head out of the carrier she's nestled in. It's an infant carrier that I have strapped to my front, and for the most part, Fish loves her outings in it.

I see her, Bizzy, Fish mewls. **She looks smart and beautiful. I can see the appeal.**

"Watch it," I tell her. More than a few women turn their head in our direction. I glance over at my mother and Georgie, and I can't help but frown. "Did you *both* have to wear a wonky quilt dress? You're inadvertently causing a scene."

It's true. Georgie has on one with blue stripes and dots,

and my mother's is a bit demurer with yellow and pink flowers.

Mom sighs. "When you run your own business, you need to be innovative when it comes to marketing. Every time we wear our own merchandise, we get stopped in the street and we practically make another sale. If you cared about us at all, you would have worn one, too."

"Why?" I hold back a laugh. "So we could look like we belong to a quilt cult?"

Fish yowls, *You look like a quilt cult regardless.*

Mom scoffs. "Don't listen to her, Georgie. We're doing the right thing. And by the way, see about making a wonky quilt cat carrier. I'd like to bring my cats out once in a while in something like that."

"*Ooh*," I muse. "That's a great idea. I want one for sure."

Georgie bumps her shoulder to my mother's. "Didn't I tell you this stuff practically sold itself?"

We load up on coffee before making our way to the back, and the petite blonde prances right over to us. Her hair is cut just shy of her shoulders, and she has fragile features and a smile that takes up half her face.

"Welcome, ladies. Are you here to join the Writing Wenches?"

"Writing Wenches?" Georgie chuckles. "I like this place already."

Mom nods. "We're here to learn how to write a novel."

So much for letting me do all the talking.

The blonde titters. "Well, this is the place to be. Most of these gals already know the basics. But if you like, I can help you outline your novel or get some ideas down. I'm Rachelle." She gasps once she spots Fish. "And who is this little cutie?" she asks, plucking my sweet cat right out of the carrier and bouncing her like a baby.

"That's Fish," I tell her. "And I'm Bizzy, this is Georgie, and that's my mother, Ree."

Georgie thrusts a turquoise business card her way. "Like what you see? Why not Rent-a-Grandma? Bizzy here is utilizing my services and you can, too—for a nominal fee, of course." Georgie quickly hands one out to all twelve women before anyone can stop her, and soon this end of the establishment is humming as they ooh and aah at the prospect of spending time with my favorite gray-haired goofball.

"Never mind her," Mom says with that ultra-annoyed look on her face she seems to reserve for her partner in wonky quilt crime.

Rachelle laughs while cooing down at my sweet cat. "It's a pleasure to meet you all—rented relatives and all. I think this little cutie can be our official mascot. Why don't you ladies take a seat, and I'll get right to helping you out."

"I'm actually okay on the writing front," I say. "But these two will need your full attention."

Georgie shoots me a look. *I see what you're doing, Bizzy Baker Wilder. But I'll have you know, I'm here to investigate, too—a potential thief trying to steal Jasper Wilder's heart.*

That makes two of us.

I make a face at the thought as I quickly land next to Hadley, and both Georgie and Mom land next to me and pull out the notebooks we brought along—each one suspiciously blank.

"Okay, ladies." Rachelle sounds like a drill sergeant all of a sudden. "Who knows what they'd like to write about?"

I give Hadley the side-eye, but she's too immersed in clicking away at her keyboard to notice me.

Mom raises her hand. "A Parisian romance. What's more romantic than a love story set in Paris?" She fans herself with her notebook, and I think she's swooning.

Fish bleats out a tiny meow. **Boy, she's got it bad. You'd better put an end to this, Bizzy, before she trots off and leaves the country.**

I nod up at the feisty feline because she's right.

I lean toward my mother. "That's a great idea. You should write about the long distance aspect of the romance. I bet it's impossible to stay romantically involved with that many miles between you."

"I'd rather not." Mom sags. "It's tough enough I have to live it."

Rachelle's mouth falls open. "You're doin' a little long distance hanky-panky? Well, there's your story. But don't put in any of that long-distance crap. This is your chance to reimagine your love story. And be sure to fill it with all the steamy romance you wish you could have with your man. It'd be a great gift to give him one day. An even better wedding present once you get the mileage between you sorted."

Mom straightens. "That's a great idea. I can really spice things up, too. I mean, we've tried to spice things up, but there are only so many naughty stories and racy pictures you can take."

Everything in me freezes. "Please tell me you have not sent that man a single racy picture."

Mom presses her lips tightly before elbowing Georgie. "What's your book about?"

Georgie's chest bucks with a silent laugh, but her expression is serious as stone. "A casino heist, a strip club, and a man with one eyebrow."

Rachelle belts out a laugh. "You've already got me hooked. Get some ideas down on paper, and I'll be back to see how you're doing." She walks down to the other end of the table with Fish in tow, and soon that tiny feline is the star of the show.

Hadley laughs as she looks my way. "Welcome to the Writing Wenches." She examines my features, and I try not to glower at the woman. She looks adorable in a denim shirt and her red hair pulled back into a whippet of a ponytail. Her lips are bright cherry red, a color I can never get away with, and yet it looks effortless on her. "Hey—didn't I meet you last night?" Her features smooth out. "Aren't you Jasper's wife?"

"That would be me." I shrug. "Guilty as charged."

She belts out another laugh. "Well, I won't lie, I sort of wish I had been charged with that same crime myself. My only crime was leaving him high and dry." She glances to the ceiling. "But I suppose he told you all about that."

My lips part, but I think better of contesting the fact.

"That's right," I say. "He told me everything."

There. At least now she'll think Jasper and I don't have a single secret between us. It's the same thing I thought right up until twenty-four hours ago.

Georgie leans in. "I don't know any of the details myself, so if either of you would like to give the kinky game away, I'd be glad to hear it."

Leave it to Georgie to kink up the conversation.

"Me too." Mom nods her way.

I filled both Georgie and Mom in on the fact I knew little to zilch on Jasper's old flame, right after I informed them that I didn't care a thing about his past.

It was right about then Fish asked me how it felt to lie to my mother.

And it felt pretty awful.

Hadley shakes her head. "I'll leave those details to Dizzy."

"It's *Bizzy*," I'm quick to correct her. "Camila just can't seem to get it right."

Hadley covers her mouth a moment. "Sorry. Camila can be a bit catty, can't she? Boy, she never liked me. Or at least it seems she didn't up until she sank her claws into Jasper herself. Anyway, what's your story about?"

"Oh, um—" Good grief, think of something quick. "It's a romance between a baker and two different suitors." I happen to have a friend out in Honey Hollow who's living the real deal. Lottie Lemon is transmundane like me, but her ability is referred to as supersensual. "She's dating both a hot judge and a hot homicide detective, and she has the supernatural ability to see the dead—mostly furry creatures who have crossed the rainbow bridge and have come back to help find the killer of their former owner."

She winces. "Wow, that's dark. Maybe go light on that whole killing thing and focus on the romance?" A goofy grin takes over her face as she sighs. "I hope you don't mind if I'm honest with you, but Jasper has been my muse for as long as I've been writing romances."

Mom and Georgie lean our way.

Georgie nods. "Go on, Toots. Fill in a couple of blanks. How exactly do you use him as your muse? I bet you named your battery-operated boyfriend after him."

Mom clucks her tongue and pulls Georgie back. "*Please*, she's a lady." She turns to Hadley. "I bet you recall all the times he gave you flowers or held your hand on a walk along the shore."

My stomach churns just thinking of Jasper doing either of those things with anyone but me. And if I'm being truthful, I'd prefer he did them with Camila over Hadley. This woman is sheer perfection. She's beautiful, intelligent, and doesn't seem to have a single screw lose. She's a triple threat.

Camila is more or less an obvious train wreck with more loose screws than the local hardware store.

Hadley leans in. "Don't think less of me, but I tend to do a bit more than that. Let's face it, Jasper Wilder is the perfect man." She fans herself with her fingers, and I can feel the breeze as well. "He's got that demanding black hair, those dreamy pale gray eyes, and when he smiles at you, it's as if you're the only woman on the planet." She groans as if she were in the throes of ecstasy, and I back up a notch in the event I decide to land a right hook.

"He is a good-looking man." Mom's brows hike, and I can tell her radar is going off with this one. *Geez, if Bizzy and Jasper we're on the outs, I'd be worried about this.* She offers me a short-lived smile. *Thankfully, I've raised my daughters to have more confidence with men than I ever did. But then, if this chick were trying to hit on my husband back in the day, she would have caught him, hook, line, and stinker. She would be the stinker, of course, even if Nathan were sort of a stinker himself. Women always seem to blame the other woman more than we do our louse of a husband. I'd warn Bizzy about this girl, but I don't want to be the one to sound the alarm. I think she might have some real trouble on her hands. And I'm not sure she's up for the challenge.*

Gee, thanks, Mom.

I turn back and force a smile as I look to Hadley. "His good looks certainly don't hurt," I say. "Go on."

"Anyway." She glances to her laptop. "I must have written six different love stories that star Jasper and me by now. They're all regency period pieces, of course. I'm big on historical romance. In this one, *The Duke and the Lady*, Jasper is the duke." She leans my way. "And I hope this doesn't make you twitchy, but I've decided to use our real names in this manuscript. Jasper is just the perfect name for that era, and well, I'm using my nickname Haddie."

"Sounds like the perfect pairing," I frown as I say it.

Georgie leans in hard and squints at the woman with suspicion. "Let me get this straight. You've already written six different romances with Jasper Wilder as your leading man?"

"That's right," Hadley freely admits.

Georgie nods my way. *This one has a pair of real cookies on her, Bizzy.*

She's got that right.

"A period romance?" I look to the woman and my eyes fall to her ruby red lips, and I wonder how many times Jasper did just that. "Sounds like a good time." A killer good time. And I'll gladly add the homicide component to this story.

"Oh, I love historical romance," she raves. "They're so much fun to write. You should take a stab at it. You could write about Jasper *and* live the dream. Jasper and I always thought we'd have a big family." Her lids lower a notch. "Well, you know. Anyway, I always give us a happy ending in each book, and I even include a little epilogue where I introduce our blooming brood. I always include Montgomery in each one. That would have been our son. And Samantha and Patrice. I always thought we'd have girls, too, one day."

"Lovely," I flatline. I don't even have names picked out for my imaginary children with Jasper. "So is that what you're working on now? The regency piece starring Jasper?"

"Yup. But I'm just nitpicking. It's all done and polished. I've even had two different editors go over it. I was about to have it done through Patterson, but things didn't turn out well for him last night."

"Patterson?" I shake my head. "Was he an editor, too?"

She shakes her head. "No, he was a publisher. But Jasper probably already knows that. He's investigating the case," she says it in such a way as if she were informing me. "If I had known he would have been there last night..." Her eyes flit to the window behind me. *I sure as hell wouldn't have chosen that night to deal with Patterson Higgins.* She blows out a steady breath. "But Jasper, well, he caught me off guard." *And I caught him off guard. I knew I was in trouble as soon as he asked the hard questions. I took one look into those starry eyes of his and I couldn't hold back. I told him the words I've always wanted to tell him. A part of me wanted to tell him for all the right reasons—but that stubborn part of me won and I told him for all the wrong reasons.* Her eyes graze over my features. *And to think this is the woman I was hoping he'd dump last night as he magically ended up in my arms once again.*

I gasp without meaning to.

"Everything okay?" She wrinkles her nose my way and looks all that much more adorable. And I can't stand her all the more because of it.

"Everything is fine," I grunt. "I just had a great idea for a historical romance myself." I frown her way. "A hardworking inn owner who finds love with a handsome homicide detective." I would've added the tidbit about my main character having the ability to read minds, but it already hits a little too close to home.

"Sounds lovely." Any trace of a smile glides right off her face. *And far too reality-based for me to be interested in.*

I thought so.

Georgie raps her knuckles over the table. "So what kinda heat level are we talking about, missy? Open doors? Closed? Fade to black with a smidge of deliciousness?"

"No fading to black for me." She giggles like a schoolgirl and my mother joins along in the chortle fest.

"Mom." I look back at the traitor.

"What? I was thinking about Romero." She tosses up a hand before busying herself with her notebook and quickly jotting down whatever trashy thoughts come to mind, I'm sure.

"Go on," Georgie is quick to spur on the flirty redhead who doesn't mind admitting to lusting after my man.

"Oh, I cover it all. There's nothing too down and dirty for me to omit." She sighs brazenly. "Boy, do I really miss his kisses." A sickly moan escapes her. "Doesn't Jasper just have the softest lips?" She looks to me and I give a circular nod in lieu of strangling her.

I take back what I said. This woman has far less brain cells than Camila Ryder. Camila might be a snake in the grass, but this woman is flying way too close to the sun.

"And that body?" She moans twice as hard. "Anyway, I spend weeks crafting our love scenes, and I make sure to include at least nine in each book."

"*Nine?*" I muse. "Sounds exhausting."

"Well, you know what a tiger he can be in bed." She claws her hand my way and lets out a roar as she laughs.

"Yes, I do." And I'm not laughing.

"Both of my editors agree that my love scenes were

some of the steamiest they have ever seen. One of those scenes goes on for forty-two pages."

"Just forty-two?" I cock a brow at the insanity of it all.

Georgie snickers. "So when can I get my hot little hands on a copy of this steamy read?"

I shoot Georgie a look. "I'm sure it's a long way from publication."

"No, no, no." Hadley waves me off. "I happen to have a few advanced copies I can give each of you. It's not the final copy. I'm still fiddling with that, but it's close. I trust you with it. I mean, it's not like you're going to swipe my work. Besides, I can use all the feedback I can get. I'm looking into self-publishing it now."

"Interesting," I say. "What was it that Patterson did again?"

"He owned Higgins House. It's a small press. He had a ton of authors working under him. He was very close to securing my contract." *And to think I was about to do that with my body.* Her cheeks turn crimson. *I'm not thrilled about what happened. Jasper made me do it. Just seeing him brought those old feelings alive in me. Too bad Bizzy is in the way. But, like Camila said, most marriages end in divorce. Come to think of it, maybe I will take Jasper up on that lunch date.*

Lunch date?

I straighten in horror. What the hell is happening?

Georgie points her way. "Is that why you offed the guy?" She winks. "Because he wasn't interested in your regency porn?"

I couldn't have phrased it better myself.

"No." Hadley looks flustered, but she laughs nonetheless. "I can assure you I had no part in his demise." ***Okay, so I had a part in it, but those words are not ever leaving my mouth.*** "If anyone had a reason to off him, it was Devan."

"Devan Abner?" I pull back because she's just caught me off guard.

She nods before taking a sip of her iced latte. "That was his ex-wife. They claim to have had one of those new agey conscious uncouplings, but the tension and the bitterness last night were palpable. Something was brewing, that's for sure. As soon as she agreed to let him choose the selection and show his face at the Grim Readers, I thought something was off. I thought to myself, *that woman is up to no good.*"

Sort of like you, I want to say but flex a dry smile instead.

"Do you think Devan was capable of murder?" I ask.

She gives a quick glance around. "Not under normal circumstances. But he was pushing her."

"In what way?"

She shakes her head. "You'll have to ask her."

"Where do you think I can find her?"

"She's a mushroom farmer." She shrugs. "Weird, right? I think she mentioned her place was out in Bramble Point. Abner Farms." She nods. "She went into business with a few of her friends. Organic mushroom farming." She makes a face. "Odd career choice. But she likes books, and that's what keeps us tethered." ***Patterson kept us tethered, too, just not in any way either of us wanted.*** She sighs as she reaches into her bag and produces three large paperbacks. "Here are those advanced reader copies I promised." She passes one out to each of us, and I take a moment to look at the cover. It's a blonde who looks remarkably like Hadley herself, and the male model looks as if he could be one of Jasper's brothers. She's wearing a corseted red dress and his hands are precariously close to second base. "I'm just dying for you to read my book."

Mom and Georgie dive right on in, and I'm tempted to do so myself.

The class wraps up, and I collect Fish before we leave.

How did it go, Bizzy? Fish mewls in my arms as we get into the car.

"It went exceptionally well, and just as terrible. But mostly terribly," I tell her.

Mom laughs. "Don't worry, Bizzy. I won't envision Jasper in all those steamy scenes as I read the book. I'll be thinking about Romero."

"Oddly, that doesn't make me feel too much better."

"Heads-up, Biz," Georgie says as we buckle up. "I'll be envisioning you and Jasper just the way God intended."

"Too bad Hadley didn't intend it to be that way."

I have a feeling I'm not going to like this book, and I haven't even hit page one.

Here's hoping it doesn't give me nightmares.

Something tells me it will.

CHAPTER 7

"*R*egency porn," I say as I close the book on my lap.

What's that? Clyde yowls as she jumps from the sofa and prances over to where Sherlock is curled up by the hearth.

Bizzy is reading about kissy stuff. Fish lashes my arm with her tail as she sits beside me. ***Jasper and Bizzy love to***

engage in it. One of these days they're going to bring a litter into this world because of it, too.

"Apparently, Lady *Haddie* beat me to it," I say.

Sherlock barks. ***Don't worry, Bizzy. My father sired many litters. I'm sure Jasper has a few more in him, too.***

"Wonderful."

I give an irritated glance around at the tiny cottage we've called home together ever since we got hitched last July. It was my cottage before Jasper and Sherlock moved in, and yet it wasn't until they took up residence here that it started to feel like a home. It's small and cozy with its frilly shabby chic curtains and a couple of yellow and white plaid sofas. There are wood floors with a fuzzy rug over them in the living room, and a simple dining room. It's not much, but it's more than enough for the two of us, and we've been happy here. Or at least I have. For all I know, Jasper could have spent his nights ruminating over Lady Haddie—the movie star that got away.

"It's as if I've been living with a stranger," I say to no one in particular and Sherlock barks.

Jasper's no stranger, Bizzy. The freckled cutie makes his way over. ***I've never seen him sniff another woman quite the way he's sniffed you.***

"Did you know Hadley?" Suddenly I'm interested in any intel Sherlock might have.

She was before my time. He rests his head on the floor and Clyde jumps up on his back. She really seems to like that position—almost as much as Lady Haddie seems to like it when it comes to Duke Wilder. Hadley was shameless in her exploitation of my husband. Or should I say *sexploitation*? **Camila brought her up a time or two, though. She was always angry about her, too.**

"Sounds as if Camila was jealous."

Sherlock gives a soft bark. **Jasper used to say that 'Jealous' was Camila's middle name.**

"Great. I wonder what he'll say about me."

Bizzy. Fish swats me with her tail once again. **Jasper adores you. He's not a tomcat. I can't see him leaving you for this lady.**

"Oh, she's no lady." A laugh rises in my throat. "Not in the traditional sense anyway. Not after what I subjected my eyes and my mind to."

The door handle jiggles and all eyes shift in that direction.

He's here! Fish yowls as she hops off the sofa and darts behind Sherlock. **Don't throw anything breakable. I'd hate to tiptoe around sharp objects.**

"Don't worry," I tell her. "A book is the best weapon for a woman in my position. And lucky for me, I've got just the literary tome."

Jasper walks in looking impossibly handsome with the scruff on his cheeks a little thicker than usual, and it only makes his eyes shine all the more like lightning.

He holds up a bag of takeout from our favorite Chinese place and offers up a lopsided smile.

"Together at last," he says, sounding a bit fatigued.

"I bet you say that to all of the women you share a meal

with." Like the lunch date he's about to have with you know who.

"What's that?" He frowns a little as he takes off his coat and heads my way. He lands a kiss to my forehead before sitting down next to me. "Hungry?"

"Not particularly."

Jasper is just about to dig into the bag when he stops midflight and his eyes flit my way.

"Why do I get the feeling I'm in trouble?"

Sherlock barks. *Because you're a smart man, Jasper. Now run to the bedroom and lock yourself in it before Bizzy breaks something.*

Jasper's lips twitch as he studies Sherlock before reverting his gaze to me.

"Why is Sherlock giving me that warning bark of his? Should I be wearing a helmet?"

Clyde belts out a sharp meow. *You're right, Sherlock. He is smart. I bet that's where you get all of your smarts, too.* She licks a line up the side of his face and a yodeling sound comes from him.

Oh, for goodness' sake. Fish sighs. *Get on with it, Bizzy, or none of us will eat tonight.*

I knew I should have fed them the minute we walked through the door.

"Bizzy?" Jasper lands the food on the coffee table and turns to face me fully.

The warm scent of his cologne makes my heart break, and suddenly I want to sob for the Jasper I knew two days ago who I didn't think was keeping a single secret from me. Not that I asked for an inventory of exes when we met. But in hindsight, I probably should have.

"How is the case?" I ask and our eyes lock a moment too long.

He shakes his head. "This isn't about the case. What's happening? Is it the inn? Did something go wrong with a guest?"

"It's very much about the case." I take a quick breath. "I questioned my prime suspect today."

"Bizzy." He inches back. "You know I don't want you doing that. I don't want you getting hurt. Who did you talk to? Where did you go?"

"Hadley Culpepper." I scowl instinctually when I say her name.

His eyes close as he lets out a breath.

"Bizzy." He takes up both of my hands. "I'm sorry. I should have made time last night to assure you she's firmly in my past. I know Camila's words must have stung."

"But you said them. I mean, if you said them once, you must have meant it. And she's *Hadley Culpepper*. I was one of her biggest fans."

"And I wasn't. When Hadley and I met, I had never even seen an episode of the show she was on."

"You were her fan for other reasons."

"And they were short-lived. We were together for a few months and then she took off."

"Is that what the two of you were arguing about last night?"

His eyes enlarge a moment before he glances to the

floor. "I'm sorry, Bizzy. I've had a tense night, a tough day, and I can't do this right now." He bows his head into his hand a moment before looking back up at me. "How about we have dinner and get to bed? I just—I'm sorry." He leans back hard against the sofa. "There's something I need to process before I tell you. But I just can't seem to push the words out right now." His lips turn down as if his emotions were about to get the better of him, and a spiral of fear shoots through me.

"Jasper, we tell each other everything—or at least that's how I've been operating. I would never keep anything from you. What's happening? If you can't say the words, think them. Don't shut me out."

He glances my way but doesn't hold my gaze.

I try my hardest to press into his mind, but I'm met with that foggy feeling as if a fortress was just tossed up to stop me.

A breath hitches in my throat. "You're intentionally trying to hold back your thoughts from me."

A forlorn smile comes and goes on his lips. "I'm sorry, Bizzy. But I just need a minute."

My heart thumps hard as if it were about to expire.

"Take all the time you want," I say as I get up. "I'm going to bed."

I fill the pets' trays with enough kibble to last a year and do just that.

But I don't sleep a wink.

CHAPTER 8

Jasper kissed me deeply this morning before he took off for the station. It was a kiss that said so much without the aid of a single word —and believe me, I appreciated the sentiment.

And even though that made me feel miles better than how we left things last night, I couldn't focus on the inn. Instead, I left it in the capable hands of my staff and recruited Georgie and Juni to use their sleuthing skills to help me track down Devan Abner. By the time I started hunting for her, she had already left the mushroom farm for the day, so I set my meager hopes on finding her elsewhere, and find her elsewhere we did—right at the Spring Festival taking place in downtown Seaview.

Pastel flags line several city blocks as thick crowds patrol the sidewalks looking at the wares that all the local businesses have to offer. It's warm out and the air feels downright swampy—far too humid for springtime in Maine. The thick scent of grilled burgers competes with the sweet scent of deep-fried blueberry fritters, and I have a sudden craving for both.

There are plenty of balloons and face painting stations for the younger set and wine and fine cuisine for the rest of us. Booths that house arts and crafts are in abundance, handcrafted jewelry glints in the late afternoon sun, and a few local bookstores have opened up outdoor samplings of their bestsellers as well. And that's the direction where we head in first.

Georgie has Sherlock on a leash and both Fish and Clyde are in my carrier.

"Don't you worry, Biz," Georgie says, giving my carrier a little pat. "By this time tomorrow, you'll have a fancy new wonky quilt cat carrier to call your own. I've already given the specs to my seamstresses."

By *seamstresses*, she means the women at the old folks home she has working as a quilting mill to create her inventory.

"Thank you," I say. "I'm actually looking forward to it."

"Tell her about the hanky," Juni says, checking her face in a compact she pulled from her purse. Juni has her game on as she put it, with her hot pink mini skirt and matching tank top. And Georgie has opted to match her daughter in a bubblegum pink kaftan. At least this way they'll be easy to spot in the event they wander away—or commit a minor felony. The latter of which is completely in their wheelhouse.

"What's the hanky for?" I ask Georgie as she scoops Clyde from my carrier.

"To sop up your tears," Georgie says, dotting a kiss to Clyde's little pink nose. "Face it, Biz, this is going to be a tough season in your life now that Jasper is taking off with that magician hussy."

"You got the hussy part right," I tell her. "Did you read that book? She had my husband twelve ways to Sunday like he was nothing more than a side of beef. And believe me, there's not a house of worship that would take her in on that sacred day either. Lusting after somebody else's husband like that makes her darn right flammable in churches worldwide."

A cute little cinnamon-colored poodle waltzes up to Sherlock and gives him a sniff from nose to tail.

Hey! Clyde belts out a rawr. *Watch where you're sniffing, hussy! Back off and find your own side of beef!*

Fish groans. *Get used to it, honey. For whatever reason, Sherlock is what Jasper calls a chick magnet.*

The poodle looks up at the tiny ginger-colored ball of

fury. *Is that a cat telling me—a dog—who I can and cannot sniff?* She barks out what sounds like a chortle before touching her nose to Sherlock's. *How about you and I find a bush and lift a leg together?*

Clyde screeches as if someone just ran over her tail and springs right out of Georgie's arms, soaring through the air like a flying squirrel, doing a couple of spins until she lands flat over the poodle's back. The dog jumps back on its hind legs doing its best to evict the cagey kitty but to no avail. Then in less than a second, the poodle darts off, followed by Sherlock—followed by Georgie.

"Cheese and rice." I cringe just watching the inadvertent pet parade as the poodle's owner takes off after them shouting a few colorful words that children probably shouldn't hear. "Don't break a hip, Georgie!" I shout. "Let go of the leash!"

"Don't worry about, Mama," Juni says, smacking me on the arm. "Check out those sides of beef hanging out in front of Bombalicious Burgers."

I glance over and spot a line of men outside of the quick serve booth situated in front of the restaurant. Behind them is the outdoor patio where couples have congregated noshing on amazing grilled sliders on what look to be a bun made of a glazed donut. Sure enough, a sign strung up over the booth reads *we bet donuts to burgers you'll love our food! Feed one to your sweetheart and you'll have a sweetheart for life! Made with real wagyu patties!*

"Ooh, wagyu," I moan at the thought. "That's some

fancy beef. And pairing it with donuts? That's just brilliant. I really want to try those."

"I'll tell you what's brilliant"—Juni grits the words in a husky voice—"that line of abs they've got showcasing their wares. Now that's some beef I'd like to wrap a donut around." She cranes her neck into the crowd. "Looks like Mama's gonna miss out on the burger buffet." She does a double take to our left. "Lookie there"—Juni knocks me in the ribs—"ain't that the perp in the orange blouse?"

Sure enough, I spot a fresh scrubbed blonde with her no-nonsense demeanor in jeans and a floral orange blouse standing under a tent filled with books. Her arms are filled with paperbacks and there's what looks to be a green smoothie in her hand.

Fish pokes her head out and looks that way. ***To choose a spinach shake in a sea of burgers swaddled in glazed donuts is pretty telling about a person.***

"I so agree," I mutter. "Juni, why don't you grab a burger and I'll go talk to Devan. I'll catch up with you soon."

We split ways and I stride over to the tent with the word *books* written across the front in bright yellow letters. It's cooler under the canopy, taking the sting of the late afternoon sun away while tinting the plethora of tables laden with books with a lime green patina. Cleverly crafted towers made of hardbacks dot the middle of the tent, erecting themselves from one end to the other like literary Christmas trees.

Devan is busy chatting away with a man in an apron

who is actively straightening the books and he points her over to my general direction.

Fish pats me on the chest. *Here she comes, Bizzy! Act natural.*

I make a left without looking where I'm going and walk right into one of those cleverly strewn literary Christmas trees, causing a slow moving avalanche that my body seems to fall right into. Lucky for Fish, I land on my side and manage to swim my way through the hardbacks to a sitting position as an entire throng of employees comes to my rescue.

Way to act natural, Fish yowls. *Are you okay? You've only got two legs, for goodness' sake. You'd better take care of them before we're both getting around on all fours.*

"Funny," I say as I nod to the kind men who help hoist me up. "Thank you so much. I'm sorry about that." I take a step out of their way as they get right to cleaning up the mess I made, and I step right into the path of Devan Abner.

A jovial laugh comes from her. "Bizzy? Is that you?" She pulls me to the side. "My goodness, are you okay? Is your cat okay?"

"I'm fine. And Fish is fine, too. My other cat is the small orange tabby, but she's actually not with me at the moment. Technically, she's not really my cat. She's sort of staying with me until we figure everything out."

"I saw her that night at the inn." She gives a wistful smile. "If you ever want to place her, you let me know. I'd love to give her a home. Are you sure you're okay?" She helps dust off my arm.

"Yup. I was just showing off some of my top klutzy moves. I'm super embarrassed."

She belts out another laugh. "Well, don't be. I've had my fair share of red-faced moments—like the time I walked right into a giant hole in the ground. My ex kept right on walking and didn't miss a beat." *Funny how the roles are reversed and I'm the one who's still walking and haven't missed a beat.*

My eyes widen a notch. "That wouldn't be Patterson, would it?" Normally, I wouldn't have segued to the deceased so quickly, but I figured since she gave me an inch I was going to take a macabre mile.

Her expression sours at the mention of him. "How did you know that?"

"Someone whispered something to the effect at the book club meeting the other night. How are you doing? Are you okay?"

"I'm fine." Her back shudders. "I still can't believe he's gone." *I'm not sorry about it, but I can't believe it. I've dreamed of this for years.*

My lips part at the horrible thought and Fish mewls.

This must be good, Bizzy. You look as if you're ready to fall right over once again.

She's not wrong.

"So how long were the two of you married?" I ask.

"Just a few years. Patterson was a pretty good basketball player in college and got recruited to the Red Claws. That's when we were together."

"Really? That's huge." The Red Claws are in the

National Basketball Association. That must be why all those women were pawing at him. They were bona fide jersey chasers.

"It would have been." She glares past my shoulder as if she was looking right at him. "But he sustained a shoulder injury to his rotator cuff that was a career ender. We were just about to move to Portland and everything. Anyway, we drifted apart. I couldn't stand the attention he was still getting from his basketball groupies, and as it turned out, he loved it. I don't know if you noticed or not, but he was still what I like to call a crowd pleaser right up until the end. Women found him irresistible."

I nod. "It was noticeable. So you must have been on friendly terms. I mean, he came to the book club you head up."

She plucks up a book off the table before us with a cartoon picture of a dog knocking over a wedding cake, and I can't help but notice there's a shiny silver knife in that pile of frosting.

"Cozy mysteries are my favorite," she whispers it as if it were a secret. "And I didn't invite Patterson that night. Technically, he invited himself. You see, years ago when we were still legally bound, he needed to come up with another way to make money since hoops were out, and as fate would have it, his uncle had a small press he was looking to offload, so eventually Patterson took over. He changed the name and Higgins House was born. He only had a handful of clients. I'm not sure whatever became of it because we split ways that summer. Anyway, fast-forward to about six months ago and he asked if I would feature one of his client's books with the Grim Readers. I looked them over and they fit the mold, so I said yes." She shrugs. "Sure, he wasn't my favorite person, but we've been amicable over the years."

"So you've featured a few books for him?"

"Three," she says it with a note of anger. "He practically begged me, but I told him this would be the last this year. My book club members were starting to talk. They wanted to vote on the books we read, and instead I was shoving books down their throats. And to be honest, the books were so-so. I'd say this last one was the best, but even still I was putting my foot down." She gives a sideways glance to a group of women laughing near the registers. "Besides, I wasn't crazy about watching my ex get hit on by a bunch of women each time he showed up. It made me uncomfortable." *And how I hated that he loved the attention. I caught those glances he cast my way as if he wanted to make sure I was witness to the spectacle. And that cheesy redhead that was dripping all over him? Lady Has Been? It's as if he especially wanted to showcase her level of ditziness to me.*

Lady Has Been? I don't doubt that she knows about Hadley's regency porn.

"Some men really like the attention from a pretty girl," I say. "I'm sorry things ended badly between the two of you."

"I'm not. That man never had any faith in me. He actually had the nerve to suggest I'd go crawling back to him one day because I wouldn't be able to make it in the world." Her expression sours. "I'm the one that busted my tail putting him through school. Once he got out and started playing in the NBA, he was going to return the favor and I was going to head to the university, but well, things didn't go that way for either of us."

Fish mewls, **She's bitter, Bizzy. Maybe she offed the man because she's not satisfied in the direction her life took?**

I graze my teeth over my lip. "So where did life take you?" I know for a fact she works at the farm, but is that where she wanted to be?

"Abner Farms"—she sets down the books in her arms and quickly manufactures a business card for me without so much as spilling her smoothie—"I bought a couple acres out in Bramble Point with my girlfriends and we grow an entire variety of organic mushrooms. Reishi, corydceps, turkey tail, chaga, shiitake, lion's mane, white button, oyster, cremini, portobello, enoki, black trumpet, and chanterelle just to name a few. I've been addicted to fungi since I was a kid, so my move to produce them was no surprise to those who knew me. We sell local, so feel free to pass the word on to the chef at the inn. I'd be glad to offer up a tour of the grounds to you anytime you'd like."

"Sounds interesting. I just might take you up on that," I say as I slip the card into my purse. "And it sounds as if you're passionate about your work. There's nothing more empowering than that. I guess you proved Patterson wrong."

"You bet I did. Right up until I asked him for a small loan." She frowns at the thought. "I even told him I'd pay him double if he'd give it to me quickly, but he said no.

Said he didn't have it himself—which I didn't believe for a minute. You don't roll around in a fancy SUV like he did and live in a house overlooking the water without having some spare change. And well, I guess the bottom line was he didn't want to spare it in my direction. As he saw it, I'm the one who left him all those years ago. He would have been perfectly happy cheating on me all the while." A dry laugh pumps through her.

He wouldn't loan her money? Fish growls up at me. *Is that a motive? I suppose one could fit in there somewhere.*

Devan clucks her tongue as she gives Fish a quick scratch. "Such a cute cat. I saw your little orange tabby there that night, too, and she about melted my heart. I had one just like her when I was a kid. Best cat ever. I keep saying we need one or twelve at the farm to keep the critters away."

Fish mewls, *Quick, give her Clyde. I'm sure she'll fall in love with the next oaf she sees.*

I swallow down a laugh. "Hey?" I look back up at Devan. "Are you thinking about rescheduling the book club? You could meet up at the inn again if you like."

She winces. "That's very nice of you, but considering how our last meeting ended, I think the venue would overshadow the event. But we're meeting up at the Cider Cove Public Library next Friday night. You're welcome to join us, and please extend the invite to your guests as well. In fact"—she plucks a paperback from her pile and shows me the cover—"this is our next selection. *The Killer Barked Twice.* It's another cozy, but the Grim Readers can't get enough of them. And the club got to pick this title, so everyone is pretty excited about it. I hope to see you there."

She starts to take a step, and I block her path.

"The sheriff's department let me know they suspect foul play in Patterson's death," I tell her.

"Oh?" She snaps up the stack of books once again. "That's terrible." Her eyes expand a touch too wide, and I can't help but think her reaction feels contrived. *So they know something? I'm shocked they haven't hunted me down by now.* "Poison, I'm guessing?" She shakes her head. "He dropped dead without a battle wound or a puncture. I've read enough mysteries to narrow the field."

"I have no idea, but you're probably right. Devan, you knew Patterson well enough. Who do you think would do something like this?"

Her lips twist as she glances out at the crowd strolling by.

A shallow part of me is hoping she'll pin it all on Hadley. Let's see how many steamy romances she can pen in prison.

Fish gives a pat on my chest. *You're rooting for Lady Haddie, aren't you, Bizzy? Don't worry. I won't think less of you. I'm rooting for Clyde.*

I make a face at the furry cutie.

"I don't know." Devan sighs. "Liv was upset that night, but she's a basket case in general. Hadley was always stomping her foot about something. But if I had to place a wager, my money would be on James Foreman." Devan nods with certainty.

"Who?" both Fish and I say in unison. Although to be fair, it was technically just me.

"His business manager, or communications whatever, I can't remember the title. Anyway, he was there that night. His old basketball buddy that he took on as an employee at Higgins House. They were arguing over something business-related. Maybe he wanted him dead?"

My mind plays back that night, and I distinctly remember a tall, lanky man in a sweater having it out with Patterson. I bet that was him.

"Sounds plausible." I shrug her way. "It was great seeing you again."

"Likewise. Swing by the library next Friday night," she says as she takes off with a wave. "And watch out for flying books!"

"Good thinking," I say as I step outside of the tent and migrate across the street toward Bombalicious Burgers where I spot Juni reunited with Georgie and they're shaking one another by the arms. I bet they're arguing over who gets to order a burger first.

Clyde is happily lounging on Sherlock's back while a little girl pets the two of them and I'm thankful everyone is back in one piece, but if I don't act fast I'm afraid Juni and Georgie might just shake one another's heads right off.

I head in their direction just as Juni holds a hand out my way, and soon enough Georgie looks my way with a look of shock.

"You can't come this way," Georgie says, darting in my direction with her hands out as if she were about to physically stop me. "I'm going to handle this for you. You're too young to do time. Besides, I've still got a felony or two left in me."

"What?"

Sherlock barks. ***Don't look, Bizzy! I just saw it myself! Quick, Fish! Turn her around. Oh, this is terrible! We've got to stop Georgie. If she heads to prison, who will feed me a steady diet of bacon? This is all Jasper's fault.***

"Jasper?" My head ticks toward the burger place and I spot his shock of dark hair, and seated across from him is a woman—a redhead who thinks of herself as a lady.

It looks as if that lunch date is still on.

"Oh no, you don't," I say, barreling my way over.

Bizzy? Fish yowls as she cranes her head in that direction and a hiss escapes her as soon as she sees the malfeasance.

"Jasper Wilder." His name rips from me as I come upon them in a blind rage.

"Bizzy?" He scoots his seat back a notch, confusion taking over his handsome face.

"How dare you step out on me with this hussy!" I say, picking up the glass of water set in front of him and dousing him in the face.

And before he can jump out of his seat, I repeat the effort with Lady Haddie's glass. Her hair flattens as she gasps and sputters, spiking out of her seat and watching me with abject horror.

"How could you?" she shrieks.

"How could *you*?" I shoot back.

"Jasper." Hadley's chest heaves and ripples and that low-cut skin-hugging dress isn't lost on me. Unfortunately, it probably wasn't lost on Jasper either. I guess that kiss we shared this morning didn't mean much to him. What I thought was a we're-going-to-make-it-kiss was obviously a very lingual goodbye.

"Jasper, do something about this," she shrieks, grabbing the glass of soda and looking my way with a threat in her eyes.

I'll handle this, Fish screeches and hops out of the carrier and onto Hadley's face.

Sherlock runs over barking at the top of his lungs while Clyde rawrs as if she has suddenly morphed into a lioness.

"Bizzy"—Jasper pulls me over—"I can explain."

"Can you?" I shout. "I don't think I need you to draw me a road map of where this was going. She was clearly trying to seduce you!"

A gasp circles us, and it's only then I note everyone here has their eyes glued our way.

Georgie and Juni break out into spontaneous applause just as Fish hops off the wench in question and the entire lot of us storms back out onto the sidewalk.

"Bizzy, wait"—Jasper catches me by the hand and spins me toward him—"we're taking care of this right now."

Hadley strides up, her face a little pink but not a scratch on her. I didn't think Fish would hurt her. She finds much more pleasure in humility.

Although I'm the one who's feeling humiliated right about now.

Hadley pants out a wry smile. "I suppose you're going to tell her." She gives a quick look to Jasper. "Go ahead." She tightens a smile my way. "I'll accept your apology in advance, Bizzy, and you don't even have to give it. I would have done the same." She softens. "He's the perfect catch." She darts into the crowd, and soon Juni and Georgie scuttle up as the three of us look to Jasper for an explanation.

He closes his eyes a moment before looking to Juni and Georgie. "Would you mind taking our menagerie and giving us a minute?"

Sherlock barks. ***No fair!***

Fish growls, ***I don't want to miss the good part, Bizzy.***

I nod up at Jasper. "Whatever you have to say to me you might as well say in front of everyone. You'll just save me the trouble from having to relay it."

Georgie leans in. "And me the trouble of listening in by way of your bedroom window. That whole glass to the ear thing doesn't really work."

Juni smacks her. "You're stuck in the Dark Ages. I've been using a stethoscope for years."

"Good thinking." Georgie smacks her back.

Jasper takes a breath and his chest expands the size of a wall. "Years ago, Hadley took off in the night, and after a few weeks of trying to get in touch with her, she let me know she moved on and that so should I. So, when I saw her the other night and asked her what that was about, she gave me some shocking news. I'm sorry, Bizzy. She caught me off guard—and then that man dropped dead. My head was spinning. And then last night, I was exhausted. And the words—they just wouldn't come."

Georgie juts her head forward. "What did she say that got you so shook up?"

Juni leans her ear his way. "She shook ya down for money, didn't she?"

Jasper looks at me with those clear gray eyes of his. "She told me that I was a father—and that she lost my baby."

CHAPTER 9

Georgie and Juni offer to take my car and the furry among us back to the inn while Jasper takes me by the hand and we find a bench under a willow tree not far from the festive melee breaking out around us.

"I'm sorry, Jasper," I say as I pull his face toward mine and run my fingers through the scruff on his cheeks. "I can't imagine how painful that was to hear."

"And for you," he says as he pulls me onto his lap. "I'll be okay. She just managed to knock me down." His eyes close a moment too long. "It got me thinking. I lost a child. I mean, I know I didn't know them or even know about them, but they existed for a moment in time, still do," he says as he looks to the sky. "And I brought that to being."

"Along with Hadley." I blow out a breath. "I feel terrible about how I behaved."

"Don't. I'm the one who feels terrible. I should never have left you in the dark."

"But Patterson died and you went straight to work. You're right, you didn't have enough time to process any of it. And on top of it all, you had a jealous wife ready to blow a hole in your chest."

He grunts as he dishes up a lopsided grin. "It's times like this I'm glad you didn't take me up on that offer to buy you a gun."

"I can feel yours on my hip. I'm a quick draw, you know."

A laugh gurgles through him. "Is that a threat?"

"I've met my limit on making good on all my threats today. The only weapon left in my arsenal is my lips. Are you still accepting kisses from them?"

"An unlimited amount." He tucks his finger under my chin and pulls me close until we share a searing kiss.

Tears come to my eyes and I blink them back. "Do you want to talk about it?"

His chest depresses as he blows out a breath. "I was thinking last night. He or she would have been about ten.

Baseball, dance classes, I don't know. It all seemed impossible to imagine. Hadley says she left as soon as she found out she was expecting. She wanted to get her bearings before she told me. But a few days afterward she ended up losing it, and that's when she decided we should both move on. It was a rather abrupt exit. I guess that's why I said what I did all those years ago—to Leo. I never said those words to Camila, but she overhead them. Anyway, it's all in the past. I've made peace with it. None of that was meant to be. Even though I would have gladly welcomed my child, I'm glad I didn't end up with Hadley or I wouldn't be lucky enough to have a hot brunette sitting on my lap right now."

A smile swims on my lips. "Glad to be at your service." My mood grows somber once again. "But, that doesn't change the fact you suffered a loss. I'm here for you, Jasper. You can grieve the child you never had the chance to know. It's okay. I'm grieving it, too."

His eyes fill with tears as he cinches his lips. "Thank you." He pulls me close and we hold one another as we watch the crowd drift by, and each child we see acts like a painful reminder of what could have been—and what will one day be for us.

Jasper wraps a lock of my hair around his finger and gives it a light tug.

He dots my nose with a kiss. "Aren't you going to ask how Patterson Higgins was killed?"

"How was he killed?"

"Death caps—poisonous mushrooms."

I gasp as I pull him in by the tie. "I know who the killer is."

🐾

"Why do I always miss all the good stuff?" Macy asks as she takes a forkful of Emmie's lobster pie and shovels it into her mouth.

It's just a few hours after that street festival fiasco and Georgie quickly relayed the conversation to Macy, my mother, my brother Hux, and Mack by proxy. I dropped by the cottage to feed Fish, Sherlock, and Clyde, and not one of them wanted to come to the shore with me. I take that back. Sherlock wanted to come, but Clyde told him he'd be staying in with her, away from any curly-haired poodles who might want to lure him into a bush.

The warm evening breeze ticks up a notch as we sit under the twinkle lights out on the patio behind the Country Cottage Café enjoying a sampling of the new menu, the lobster pie to be exact. It's just buttery lobster mixed with heavy cream, sitting in a decadent piecrust with bread crumbles on top. It's rich, creamy, and dreamy to the point of no return.

I moan through a bite as I point my fork over at my sister. "None of what happened this afternoon was good. And all of you have to swear you won't say a word to Jasper about it." I'm not too thrilled Georgie shared the details of his loss to begin with, but I suppose she needed to quantify all that screaming about Jasper not cheating on me once we arrived.

Juni went to close up Two Old Broads and Mom ran out of there like a bat in heat, so I offered her dinner and she took me up on it. Macy and Hux were already here, so we thought we'd stage an impromptu intervention concerning that international boy toy she met on that dicey app geared for seniors, Dating Not Waiting.

As soon as Jasper dropped me off, he went straight back to Seaview. He's going to track down Devan Abner to have a chat with her, along with seeing about getting a warrant to search her mushroom farm.

A poisonous mushroom.

I can't believe someone cooked down enough fungi to create a toxin and slipped it to Patterson Higgins that night. Jasper said toxicology was able to pinpoint that it came from a specific mushroom called a death cap.

Funny, I didn't hear Devan rattling off that name in the roll call of fungi she gave me earlier. It's probably a part of her private reserve. At least we were able to narrow down the killer relatively quickly this time. And that gets Jordy off the hook. Although I will admit, it all feels anti-climatic at this point. Usually there's a bit more fanfare when it comes to catching a killer. But that doesn't mean James Foreman is off the hook. I still need to conduct my due diligence and ask him a few questions.

Behind us the crowd of tourists has steadily grown and so has the line at the outdoor grill. As thrilled as I am to see the café churning out the extra revenue, it pains me to see people waiting in long lines for their dinners. I think I'm going to double my chefs for tomorrow night.

"Go ahead, Huxley." Mom frowns over at my brother as he fiddles with her phone. "You're not going to find anything fishy."

Hux shakes his head. "I said he could be phishing you. *Cat*fishing. It means he's misrepresenting who he is because he wants something—most likely money."

Macy bumps her elbow to my mother. "You haven't given him any money, have you?"

Mom's eyes widen a notch, and that tells us everything we need know.

The rest of the table groans her way.

"I need more ice chips." Mackenzie rattles her glass and Emmie is quick to comply. "And why is there so much seafood here tonight?" She covers her mouth with her hand and Emmie helps her to the next table over where Mackenzie sinks her head between her legs.

With the naked eye you can hardly tell that Mackenzie is knocked up, but her never-ending nausea serves as a reminder to all, especially her.

"I'm never sleeping with you again," Mackenzie shouts at my brother as she groans hard. "You stay away from me with that power stick."

"Power stick?" Georgie barks out a laugh. "Hear that, Ree? That's what the kids are calling it these days."

Macy leans toward my mother. "As much as I very much look forward to driving a stick shift tonight, let's get back to that whole money thing. Mom, you didn't hand this guy my inheritance, did you?"

Mom balks at the thought. "You kids really think I have the word *gullible* printed on my forehead, don't you?"

"Nah." Georgie sinks her fork back into her lobster pie. "They just think you're randy and anxious to give it all away to the first good-looking set of abs that comes along."

Mom bounces with a silent laugh. "Worse yet, they don't even think he exists!"

"How much did you give him?" Hux asks, wagging her pink glitzy phone case over at her.

"None of your beeswax," she's quick to counter. "And give me that." She starts to swipe her phone and he pulls it out of her reach.

"Come on, Mom," Hux says. "Just give me your password into the dating app so I can read these exchanges you claim are innocent and we'll all go away."

Mom glowers over at her only son. "I'm certainly not letting my children read the private conversations I've had with my boyfriend. Don't the three of you have love lives? You wouldn't want me nosying around in your text messages, would you?"

"You could read mine with Jasper," I volunteer.

Georgie rolls her eyes. "Ree, let the kid into your account. It's clear you need to do a little modeling. The girl is having G-rated conversations with her husband."

Mom scoffs with a laugh. "Hand over your own phone, Toots. Mine is off-limits." She takes a breath as she surveys us all. "And if you must know, I simply loaned him six hundred dollars. It was all done on the up and up on that Venmo, or Bevmo app you kids use. His wallet was stolen while he was at the beach, and he needed the money for food and incidentals. And before you start—he didn't ask for the money, I insisted."

We give another collective moan, although with a little more oomph this time.

Hux shakes his head. "Mom, you're a conman's dream. I forbid you to give him another dime."

"Or what?" she muses.

"Or I'm going to tell Dad," Hux says with a stern look and Mom laughs right in his face.

"Your father and I have been divorced almost as long as we were married. You won't have to tell him. I'm having lunch with him and Gwyneth tomorrow, I'll tell him myself."

Gwyneth would be Jasper's mother. Yes, I know. It's odd to have my mother-in-law also play the part of my stepmother, but what will really be awkward will be the divorce. With every subsequent marriage my father has, it seems his tolerance for the union only grows shorter. Jasper and I are not looking forward to the fallout.

Mom looks my way with a short-lived smile. "So who's next on your hit list, Bizzy? Got any suspects you'd like me to track down? Where's the investigation taking you next? Edison? Bar Harbor?"

"France?" Macy gives a greedy grin to my mother because she just bested her at her own game. "Changing the subject won't work."

Mom nods at her oldest daughter as if the game was on. "Where to, Biz?"

"I don't know. I'm hunting down a man by the name of James Foreman. He's tall, dark hair, used to play basketball in college, I'm assuming, and he works at the deceased's publishing house."

A lusty moan comes from Macy. "I'm in. I say we hunt this man down tonight." She wastes no time in clicking at her phone and Mom chuckles.

"I'm a pro," Mom says, winking over at Georgie.

"So am I." Hux lets out another hard groan as he holds my mother's phone an arm's length away. "You sent him nudie pictures?"

"Give me that!" Mom snatches her phone back with ease, but only because Hux all but surrendered it. "Those are tasteful pictures from the waist up—and there might be a few of my backside."

Mackenzie retches from the next table over and about six different people run for cover.

Emmie nods my way. "I'll take Mack for a walk along the waterline. Cooling off her feet might help."

"Why did you have to say feet?" Mackenzie grumbles as the two of them stagger toward the sand.

"I'm not nude in those pictures. I'm covering my nipples with my arm," Mom protests in an effort to maintain her integrity.

Little does she know that went out the back along with her derrière.

Hux points a finger her way. "Delete those. The last

thing we need is him threatening to sell them."

"Romero would never do that." She hugs her phone to her chest. "You don't know him the way I do."

Hux takes a breath. "I know him enough to realize he's going to need more money."

"And so what if I give it?" Mom tosses up a hand. "It's my life. And by the way, no—I don't plan on sending him another dime, or another picture."

Macy nods. "At this point, any more photo inspections might be a liability on your part. Good thinking using your hands as a bra. That can give the girls just the right lift to make them look as perky as ever."

Mom ticks her head to the side. "Well, I wasn't born yesterday. There's a reason I chose that pose."

"Mom"—I tap my fork to my plate—"do you have a picture of this man?"

"I sure do." She fiddles with her phone and flashes it our way and the entire table is stunted into silence.

"Holy guacamole," Georgie pants. "I gotta get myself on that dating app."

"Holy power stick, Batman." Macy's jaw unhinges and I think she just drooled. "He's freaking hot."

She's not wrong. Staring back at us is a picture of a shirtless muscle man with tan and oiled abs that glisten in the sun as he relaxes under a palm tree.

"What?" Mom balks once again as she powers down her phone. "You don't think I'm capable of landing a man half my age and twice as good looking, do you?"

Hux shakes his head. "Mom, it's not that. It's just—that's

obviously a fake picture. It's a stock photo. I'll be able to prove it in a hot minute."

Mom rises in a huff and grabs her purse in haste. "I'm leaving now. You know it's funny how nobody batted a lash when your father brought home an entire parade of bikini-wearing twenty-somethings—Bambi, Barbie, and Betty Boop to name a few. I'll just let you chew on that."

She takes off and we let out a collective breath.

"How do you like that?" I say. "Mom just served up a side of guilt to go with that lobster pie."

Hux knocks out that last bite on his plate before swallowing it down. "It doesn't change the fact she's being taken for a ride. Keep me posted, would you? Thanks for dinner, Biz. I'd better get Mack home and try to get some dinner in her, too." He gives my sister and me a quick embrace, lands a kiss to Georgie's cheek that leaves her swooning, and then takes off for the sand.

"Well, ladies"—Macy says, gathering her purse—"I don't know about you, but I've got a hot date out in Edison tonight."

Edison is the sleazy town adjacent to Cider Cove where nothing but toil and trouble happens. It's wicked, vile, and full of thugs.

"There's no way I'm letting you go to Edison tonight," I tell her. "It's bad enough I have to worry about our mother."

"Oh really? And here I thought you'd offer to drive. That hot date is with James Foreman at a club called The Right Stuff."

I gasp as I quickly grab my own purse. "If we hurry, I'll get one last suspect to quiz before Jasper closes out the case."

"Yeehaw!" Georgie hitches her thumb to the sky. "If all goes well tonight, I might land me a man of my own who'll need me once he loses his wallet."

I nod her way. "Something tells me the odds are in your favor."

Macy bleeds a dark smile. "And if all goes well for me tonight, I'll be driving a power stick back to my place."

Something tells me we'll all find what we're looking for over in that wicked, vile town full of thugs and one shiny new suspect.

Edison, here we come.

CHAPTER 10

The address James Foreman gave my sister leads us to the downtown district of Edison, straight into a lux high-rise hotel called the Royal Regency.

"The penthouse?" I muse as the elevator spits us out onto polished marble floors and we find a couple of bodyguards standing outside of a gilded door while a mob of beautiful women all clamor to get inside. And now those guards will have to contend with Macy, Georgie, Juni, and me as well.

"That's right." Macy blows on her fingernails before buffing them over her chest. "Nothing but the best. This guy is the real deal. He's got some serious change rolling around in his pocket, and he's a looker. We're talking Wolf of Wall Street material."

"If my memory serves correctly, he was dressed more like the guy who does the taxes of those wolves." It's true. He was tall, lanky, and cozy in a sweater. Devan said he has some position at the publishing house Patterson Higgins was running. She said they were arguing over something business-related, and that's as good as a motive for me.

Georgie chuckles. "If Jasper asks what you did tonight, just tell him you were running with the wolves."

Juni sucks in a breath as she looks to the woman who bore her. "There's a full moon tonight, Mama. How about when we finish up here we head out and run with the pack just like the old days?"

Macy scoffs. "You can run in the woods. I'll be running wild in the bedroom."

"And this is why I drove," I say. "And don't worry, Georgie. I won't need an alibi when it comes to my husband. If Devan and her magic mushrooms turn out to be a dead end—pun intended—then I'll be one step ahead of the game. Besides, I'm not investigating. I'm merely making sure my sister doesn't get ravished by a wild animal." I blink a smile her way. "Now get us through that door."

We scuttle onward with Macy as our fearless leader. Macy, Juni, and I have all donned the requisite little black dress—as have the masses congregating around those beefy security guards. And Georgie has stayed true to herself, wearing a lime green kaftan with white paw prints all over it.

Macy elbows her way to the front of the line and gives one of the bald walls of muscle her name, and soon the gilded door is opened and she's escorted inside.

Georgie, Juni, and I go to follow, but the door is promptly shut in our faces.

"Sorry, ladies." The wall of muscles gives a consolatory smile. "Feel free to join the kitty collective." He nods to the mob of women behind us. "If there's an opening, we'll let you know."

"What?" I pull out my phone to text my flaky sister when the gilded door opens once again and Macy stands there like a queen with yet another security guard by her side. "Great," I mutter. "They're giving her the boot already."

Juni groans. "That's too bad because I smell men and money, two of my favorite flavors, and I was really starting to get a bad craving for both."

"Eh." Georgie shrugs. "I've got a couple of men on a pint of ice cream in the freezer. Come on over and we'll drop a quarter in it and make it taste like money for you."

"Just like the good old days, Ma," Juni muses.

Macy points in our direction, and soon Mr. Muscles navigates us inside and shuts the door behind us.

"How do you like that?" I muse. "And here I thought they were showing you to the door," I say to Macy as we step into the palatial penthouse suite. Marble floors, brass hardware, crystal chandeliers. It looks like a hotel within a hotel. Classical music floats through the air, and the scent of something sweet layered with copious amounts of cologne takes over our senses. The foyer opens to a grand room to our right with a plethora of round tables set out. Each one is covered with green felt and has at least ten men seated around it playing a game of cards.

Chips rise like mini mountains in front of a few of them, short crystal tumblers bearing dark brown liquor are staggered about, and I can see a bona fide bar to the right. A small army of women in short black dresses and tiny white aprons run to and fro with trays full of cocktails, and a handful of women are scattered among the men at the tables.

"Is this some illegal gambling outfit?" I hiss Macy's way just as a tall redhead with one of those tiny white frilly aprons tied around her waist comes our way.

"It's high stakes poker. It's not illegal." She winks over at me. "And you're late." She quickly hands Georgie, Juni, and me an apron, but Macy outright refuses.

"I'm here on a date," Macy says, pointing toward the expansive floor-to-ceiling windows that look like a glassy black wall at this time of night. "I see James over there. I'd better rub up against him. I hear it brings good luck into the world." She winks my way as she takes off.

"I hear it brings babies into the world, too," I call after her, but she just waves me off.

My sister is no stranger to dating one of my suspects. She's always been one to live on the edge. Not even the time she was almost hacked to death by a killer has managed to deter her. Macy is the Unsinkable Molly Brown version of the dating world. Only I think her nickname would be the *Unkillable* Macy Baker. It doesn't have nearly the same ring to it, but she's still alive, so there's that.

"It won't bring babies into the world for me, Toots." Georgie balls up her apron and hands it right back. "I'm here to play with the big boys and not a babe will come of it." She's about to take off then backtracks and looks at the redhead. "Hey, you got any kids?"

The redhead looks momentarily perplexed—an expression that she'll grow quite familiar with by the end of the night now that the Cider Cove Circus has arrived. And yes, I know, I've included myself in that menagerie.

"I got three," she says. "One in high school and two in college. Why do you think I took on this gig?"

"Good." She slips her a business card. "My Rent-a-Grandma rates are half off this month only, so you'd better act fast."

"Aww," the woman coos down at the card. "I really miss my grandma. This is wonderful. Would you mind if I took you to breakfast and afterwards we went garage saling? Those were the days, I tell you."

"I just had Saturday morning open up. You're a lucky

one, Red. Ring me and we'll have the time of our lives. But for now, I drink champagne and roll my chips with the best of 'em," Georgie says as she ducks into the next room.

"Go get 'em, Grandma!" Red shouts and Juni and I exchange a look.

There's a frenetic energy buzzing in the air, something electric that lets you know something exciting is happening here tonight, that much I can't deny.

"All right, girl, chop-chop." The redhead motions for us to get with it, so I quickly tie my apron around my waist, but Juni looks as if she needs a little more convincing.

Juni snorts. "Why do they get the men and *champs*, and I get stuck serving bubbly?"

The redhead chuckles. "You girls are serving dessert. I don't let newbies serve the good stuff. But lucky for you, the banana pudding is good stuff, too." She shuttles us into the kitchen in the back where an entire infantry of chefs look as if they're losing their minds. And soon, Juni and I are each handed a tray with dozens of Mason jars filled with banana pudding—Nilla Wafers pressed up against the glass with luscious layers of vanilla pudding topped with whipped cream and colored sprinkles as if this were going out to a bunch of eight year olds at a birthday party. Each one has a silver spoon spiked in it, ready and rearing to land in some lucky man—or woman's mouth. There might only be six women here, but I'm sure as heck going to make sure they indulge in this sweet treat, too.

Juni and I head back onto the floor and offload as many of the sweet treats as we can. I don't come across a single rejection and lose nearly half my inventory as I make my way toward that dark row of windows where I see Macy all but crawling into James Foreman's lap. There he is, looking as tall and lanky as ever, but tonight he's traded that sweater for a three-piece suit and looks every bit that wolf that Macy warned us about.

"Evening," I say as I come to the table, and each of the men quickly snaps up one of my desserts. "Macy?" I hand one her way and she wrinkles her nose at it.

"No thanks," she's quick to be the first to reject it. *I would kill to dive into a vat of that right now. But the last thing I need to do is clue James in on the fact I eat. I have a strict no noshing on dates policy I need to adhere to. I haven't broken it in thirteen years, and I'm not going to start tonight.*

I make a face as I hand one to James, and he blindly accepts before sorting through his cards once again. He's handsome more or less, definitely the body of a basketball player with his long arms and frail neck. His dark hair swoops to the side, and he's doused himself with enough cologne to become a human blowtorch if so much as a spark hits him.

"And one for you, Macy." I plop one in front of her. "Extra sprinkles, just the way you like it."

A hard moan comes from her as she eyes it.

"Oh, what the hell." She plucks the spoon out, and no sooner does she shovel in a bite than she expels a hearty moan.

James quirks a brow her way. *Now there's some music to my ears. I might have to take a monetary loss and cut out early. It'll be worth it just to hear her sing like that in my bedroom. I wonder what I've gotta do to make that happen?*

"Not a lot," I mutter. "You'll never have an easier time getting lucky."

"What's that?" He glances up my way.

"Oh, I said there's not a lot of dessert left, so you're one of the lucky ones."

"Ah," he says as someone shouts something from the head of the table, and soon everyone is tossing their cards into the middle, and a man to my right is raking all the chips his way. "I'm diabetic, I can't have it. Sorry. Maybe see if there are any other takers."

A few of the men get up and stretch their legs, and as soon as the seat next to him grows vacant, I fall into it.

"Thanks," I say. "Maybe I'll just take a bite myself. It looks that good. "Diabetic, huh? I'm sorry about that. It must be tough to be around sweet treats all the time."

"Nah." He shakes his head. "The sugar-free stuff is just as good. It's the liquor I miss."

"No liquor?"

"Nope. Not a drop. I haven't touched the stuff in years. But that was purely my choice. If I knew how to handle my liquor, I could partake a little here and there, but I'm an all-in kind of a guy so I've made a promise to myself to stay away from the stuff. It takes discipline, but it can be done." He picks up a crystal goblet and hoists it my way. "Diet soda." He winks as he takes a sip. "Keeping my wits about me is what keeps me winning."

Macy moans again as she takes another bite.

"Mmmwatisinheremm?" she garbles out the word and I simply shoot her a short-lived smile.

"I'm Macy's sister," I fess up. "I work clubs like this once in a while because the tips are so good." The lie spills from me effortlessly.

"Oh, here." He leans over and quickly produces a wad of bills. "That was rude of me. Thank you." He shoves the money into my hand before I can protest.

"Wow, thank *you*," I say as I tuck the small wad into the pocket of my apron.

"Take this, too." He slides the banana pudding my way.

"I'm pretty sure the kitchen staff will toss it," I say. "The kitchen has a strict no regifting food policy." That would be the kitchen at the Country Cottage Café, but James doesn't need to know that.

"In that case, why don't you help yourself? I hate to see food go to waste. I grew up with a single mom and she taught us *waste not, want not*."

"Well, if you insist," I say, digging the spoon a notch deeper before indulging in a bite myself and oh my—

I see stars—heck, I can *hear* "The Star-Spangled Banner" playing in my head.

"Oh, geez!" I give a hard moan. "This is fantastic." I look over at Macy and she gives a frenetic nod. "I'm going to have to get the recipe." I glance over at James. "I work at the Country Cottage Inn as well. They're pretty much known for their delicious desserts."

"The inn over in Cider Cove?" He straightens in his

seat. "You weren't there the night of the book signing last week, were you?"

"The night that man dropped dead?" I tip my ear his way. "Sure was. How about you?" I wouldn't have left it so open-ended if I thought he might try to lie about it, but there's an inherent honesty about him.

I should lie. He frowns down at the table. "Yup. I was there. That was my boss, the man who passed away."

"Patterson Higgins?" I feign shock. "I mean, he had such a memorable name, I couldn't forget it."

"That was him." His chest puffs up a moment. "He was decent guy. Had some quirks. Had a publishing house, that's where I'm at right now." *Lord knows I should cut and run, but I'd hate to leave the place in disarray. I should have cut and run a long time ago.*

"What's going to happen to the publishing house?"

"I have no idea. I'm in talks with the city to see if they can help me figure out what to do. It might take a court order and some legal counsel, but I think the authors can receive what funds are due to them and I'm assuming they'll get their publishing rights back." *Not that there's anything due to those poor schmucks.*

Did he just call the authors *poor schmucks*?

"Was Patterson a successful publisher?" I shake my head as if I already know the answer.

He winces. "He was. If you count his profit as a marker for success, you could say he was a very successful publisher. The authors didn't fare so well, but as Patterson used to say, 'It's just the luck of the draw.'" **And a slim to nothing advertising budget.**

Slim to nothing advertising budget…

"A friend of mine is a writer. She's shopping her novel right now. Regency romance." It takes everything in me not to gag.

"Romance—that's what keeps the publishing wheels spinning." He gives a wistful shake of the head. "I'd say sixty percent of what we sell at Higgins House is romance."

"Oh? What's your role there?" I ask as Macy's eyeballs roll into the back of her head and she lets out another hearty moan.

This girl. James gives a sly grin her way before reverting his attention back to me. *I'd better play nice with the sister.*

He leans back in his seat. "I'm the communications manager. And believe me, I've spent the last week doing a heck of a lot of communicating. But the authors all seem to understand. There are about six hundred authors as it stands, so I sent off a mass email. Some wrote back and asked about rights, so I had to henpeck my way through those while responding. It's all up in the air, but everyone is being as understanding as can be." *Here's hoping I can transfer the title to the company to myself. I asked Pat a year ago if I could be a full-fledged partner, but he balked at the idea. But I'd like to think he'd be happy with the outcome.* He sheds a quiet laugh. *He should have listened to me a year ago, and if he did, he might be alive today.*

Might be alive today?

"I'm glad they were so understanding," I say. "Did Patterson have any disgruntled clients?"

A loud yelp of a laugh bursts from him. "About six hundred of them." He chuckles as he downs the rest of his soda. "Let's just say Patterson was good at one thing and one thing only, making promises."

"So he had a lot of irate clients?" The buzz starts to build at the table once again as the seats fill in, and it looks as if the seventh-inning stretch is just about over. "Did you know that the sheriff's department thinks Patterson was murdered?"

"Oh yeah." He gives a quick glance around. "I had the lead homicide detective come by the publishing house office earlier. Decent guy, nosy as hell, but I guess that's his job. He let me know someone spiked Patterson's drink."

So much for having inside intel just because I'm sleeping with the lead homicide detective. Jasper made no mention of the fact he was going to speak with James.

"Yup." He nods. "For all I know, he could still be at the office." He checks his phone.

He's at the publishing house office! That means *I* could be at the publishing house office.

James nods. "I let him look at the company register from the last year. Just things I had access to. Meetings we had, a few conference calls, authors we were courting, that's about it. Not much to see there."

"Had you been to the book club before that night? I mean, it seemed interesting."

He shrugs. "Not as interesting as you would think. But

yes, I've been so often I'd like to consider myself a full-fledged member of the Grim Readers." A tiny smile plays on his lips. *In fact, I look forward to our next meeting where I will finally have Ms. Hadley Culpepper to myself.*

A breath gets caught in my throat and I hold it.

Hadley? He wants Hadley? Oh wow, he can have her. Who knows? If things go well, he might even get to star in her next novel.

Any trace of a smile quickly fades from his lips. *Patterson was always in the way with that one. He thought she was falling in line like the rest of them. He was just too blinded by his own greed to see the light.*

"Game," someone shouts from the head of the table, and soon the original owner boots me out of my seat.

"It was nice talking to you," I tell him.

"Likewise," he says as the cards are dealt his way.

Macy tells me to scat by way of waving me off with her fingers, and I spot Georgie across the room in her lime green kaftan so I head her way. She's seated at a table with eight men and is guarding her cards with the best of them.

"Not now, Biz. I'm looking to win big in this round." Georgie motions to a small mountain of chips in front of her. "I've already taken half the loot, and I'm not leaving until I get the rest of it." She glances my way. "Don't just stand there. More banana pudding. It's my secret weapon."

"Your wish is my command." I lean in. "You've got five minutes. We have to get moving."

"I need an hour," she says, shuffling her cards.

"An hour?" I mutter and I rush into the kitchen and toss

a banana pudding at everyone in my path, including everyone at Georgie's table.

When in Rome.

I spot Juni sitting on a sofa just behind the table noshing on her own banana pudding, so I pluck two off my tray and head her way. I need to get Juni, collect Georgie far sooner than an hour, and get to Higgins House Publishing stat if I want a chance to snoop around with Jasper.

"We need to get going," I tell her.

No sooner do I take a seat next to Juni than a thought hits me.

"What's the matter?" Juni grouses. "Mama stole your man, too?" She dips her spoon back into her banana pudding and dishes herself a creamy scoop.

"No." My lips part as I look across the room as James whispers to my sister and she gives a giddy laugh. "Oh my word," I pant as I look directly at that dark-haired man that's beguiling Macy and groan.

James Foreman looks my way, and for a solid moment we lock eyes and a chill rides through me as if I've just looked at the Devil himself.

"He lied," I whisper as James gives his attention back to the cards in front of him.

"Oh hon, that's what men are best at. Don't take it personally. It's sort of a survival mechanism with them."

"He said he didn't have the wine," I breathe the words out lower than a whisper. "And I distinctly remember him standing in line to get a glass full—and then walking around with it." Oh, he lied right to my face. But if he's diabetic like he said he is, then he could have very well poisoned the wine and gave it to Patterson—and that would leave him alone with both the publishing house *and* Hadley. "On second thought, we'd better stick around a minute while I process things." I shove a heaping spoonful of banana pudding into my mouth in hopes to do just that.

My phone bleats and I fish it out. It's a text from Jasper.

At Higgins House Publishing. In the mood to hop down and join me?

I text right back. **I would, but I'm stress eating banana pudding at the moment. And I think I'm staring right at the killer!**

Bizzy. He shoots back before those dancing ellipses go off again. **Where are you? Never mind. Get out now. Run. Text me when you're safe in the car. On second thought, drive home then text me.**

I indulge in another few bites as quickly as I can.

"Mmm, this really is good," I muse to Juni just as my phone bleats again.

I know you well enough to know you're not leaving until you're good and ready. For my sanity's sake, please just tell me where to find you.

Juni grunts, "Tell the poor man where you are. It's not like they're going to let him in."

"Fine."

In Edison at the Royal Regency, penthouse. Some high stakes poker club. Don't worry. It's all perfectly legal.

He texts right back. **The Right Stuff???**

"How about that?" I muse to Juni. "He knows exactly where we are."

My phone bleats again. **Bizzy, get out NOW. That's a notorious mob hangout. I assure you nothing in the penthouse is legal!**

"Exclamation points and caps?" Juni clucks her tongue "It looks to me someone's got a temper."

"A mob hangout?" I hiss as I look around at the dapper gentlemen and their wicked grins with new eyes. "We need to get Georgie and Macy. We need to get out of here fast."

My phone bleats in my hand again, and I land the pudding on the table next to me.

Who's the killer, Bizzy?

I make a face at the phone. **In the event I don't make it out of here alive—the killer is James Foreman.** I hit send with a touch too much determination and nearly knock the phone out of my hand.

"Come on," I say, burying my phone back into my purse and grabbing Juni. "It's time to make tracks."

We head over to Georgie's table, only to find her kaftan crumpled up in a ball on the table and a couple of Nilla Wafers stuck to the outside of her bra.

A hard groan comes from me. "Georgie," I hiss. "Get those cookies off your brassiere."

"Hon, I'm not wearin' a brassiere. These days I only wear that boulder holder on days that end in Z."

"GAH!" I snatch her up and pull that dress off the table, spraying chips around errantly and a dusting of cards, too.

The men spike out of their seats in a revolt, and in the process the table jostles and a couple of Mason jars tip over, making an instant mess over the area.

"Food fight!" Georgie shouts, picking up her spoon and slinging banana pudding at the man across from her. And within seconds, banana pudding is being flung every which way.

"Good grief!" I shout as I toss her dress over her head. "We need to go, *now*." I drag both her and Juni across the way, getting pegged in the neck, the leg, and square over my bottom—you can't tell me someone wasn't aiming to get that shot.

Laughter breaks out, as do errant howls as perfectly reasonable looking men—or mobsters as they might be—continue to sling banana pudding at one another as if they had suddenly reverted back to seventh grade.

I tiptoe over to Macy while James flicks a few shots off at a nearby table and shouts something about teaching them a lesson for stealing his lunch.

"Come on, Mace"—I say as I pull her my way a few inches—"we need to leave now. Jasper says so."

"I don't care what Jasper says." She yanks her hand back. "He's your boss, not mine. I've got a stick shift to drive, if you know what I mean. I'm not looking to sit in the back seat of your used car while your hubby dictates our every move."

I pull her in close by the shoulders in one hulkish move. "That man whose lap you've been seated in all night? I think he just might be the killer!"

A yelping noise emits from her. "Why didn't you say so?"

Macy rockets us to the door and I drag Georgie and Juni along with me.

"Wait!" Juni cries out above the shouting and the salty language flying behind us. "I need me some more banana pudding."

"Good idea," I say. "We'll raid the kitchen first."

We make a mad dash that way and scoop up as many Mason jars as our arms will allow and we hightail it out of that penthouse into the first open elevator, and out of the Royal Regency as if it were on fire.

I don't text Jasper. Instead, I drive like a madwoman all the way back to Cider Cove, and about halfway there I find a familiar car following me.

"We're being tracked. Lose him, Biz!" Georgie shouts. "You hit the gas, I'll pelt him with banana pudding."

"It's Jasper," I tell her. "He's just making sure I'm safe."

Macy snorts. "First, he tells you what to do and then he tails you? I think you've got a problem on your hands, little sister. And this possessive behavior is precisely why I'm never getting hitched."

Juni turns to Georgie. "Macy got the brains."

"I've got brains," I mutter. Enough brains to know that this case has two very viable suspects—Devan and James. And, of course, Hadley, too. I can't let her off the hook. She wrote regency porn about my husband.

Fine, she underwent a trauma I know nothing about. I guess I have to give her a pass all the way back to 1812.

After dropping everyone off, I pull into the driveway and Jasper pulls up behind me. I get out and quickly hand him his very own banana pudding.

"I guess I'll have to return the Mason jars to the hotel or it's considered stealing." I cringe. "But something tells me petty theft is the least of my worries."

He nods. "You could have been killed."

"Yeah, but instead of bullets, those mobsters shoot with banana pudding," I say, plucking at a strand of my sticky hair.

His brows furrow a moment as the moonlight kisses his features and turns his hair a pale shade of blue.

"I think you have some pudding right there." He brushes his finger over my neck before diving in and cleaning it off with his kiss. Jasper pulls back and his chest expands with his next breath. "Let me help you get cleaned up."

"Wait—what happened when you questioned Devan?"

His shoulders sag. "She swears up and down she doesn't grow anything toxic. I put in a request with the judge for a search warrant of both her home and her business, but she assured me I wouldn't find anything."

I scoff. "That's because by the time you get your hands on those warrants, her hands would have disposed of the evidence—that is, if she did it. And if she didn't…"

He nods. "Someone could be trying to frame her."

"And what about our diabetic killer?"

"Let's hope he doesn't skip town before I can question him again. Higgins House checked out. He let me have the run of the place but only as far as he had access himself. Nothing shady on the outside. But as for now, I'm clocking off. I've got a wife to tend to. The killer will have to wait."

"In that case." I pull three more Mason jars full of banana pudding out of the car. "How do you feel about food fights?"

A dark laugh brews in his chest. "I think we're both going to come away victorious in this war." He leans in and touches his lips to my ear. "I'll make sure of it."

And a delicious time is had by all.

Patterson Higgins' killer will have to wait.

For now.

CHAPTER 11

"I'm ruined!" Mom wails as she hugs Clyde tightly.

It's the middle of the afternoon, the day after the banana pudding wars, and my mother summoned Jasper and me down to her shop, Two Old Broads.

Georgie and Juni are here snickering by her side while petting Fish and Sherlock.

"And you can't tell your siblings." Mom gives me a stern look that amounts to a death threat.

Two Old Broads is an eclectic little shop that sells wonky quilts in all its configurations. The store is as cozy as can be with its red painted doors that lead inside and its pastel walls and rustic wood floors. There's a candle burning on the checkout counter and the entire place is permeated with the scent of lavender.

Not only do they sell candles and knickknacks, and a few of Georgie's art pieces, but by and large they sell quilts in every configuration. But as fate and the upper eighties temperatures outside would have it, there's not a very big market for blankets this time of year. Last month, they filmed a show, put it out on the internet, and experienced a spike in sales, but that seems to have dropped off, too.

"Mom"—I gently grip her by the shoulder—"what happened?" I don't bother telling her that I've already texted Macy and Hux. I couldn't help it. She called in hysterics telling me she was being robbed at gunpoint and that she needed both Jasper and me to get the culprit. Of course, my siblings are going to be concerned. "Just start from the beginning."

"Most of this is Camila Ryder's fault." Mom gives Clyde a rather furtive kiss on her furry little forehead.

"What?" Jasper and I say in unison.

"You heard me." She looks at Jasper accusingly. "It was that *ridiculous* show of hers. She's spotlighted Romero and me *twice,* calling us the next natural disaster to hit Cider

Cove. She's glommed on to that whole catfishing idea you and your siblings put in her mind."

My mouth falls open. "Mom, did Camila rob you at gunpoint? How does she factor into this?"

"She might as well have." She scoffs. "After she put out that information, some loon must have hacked into Romero's computer and then I woke up this morning to this email." She taps into her phone before handing it my way.

"Attention, Ms. Baker"—I read out loud for all to hear, and considering there are no customers in here at the moment, nobody is objecting—"I have obtained thirteen nude photos of you. I am sure you would not want these to fall into the wrong hands. That would be very embarrassing for your family and friends. If you were my mother, I would want you to buy them all back. These pictures are safeguarded with me right now. But if you don't send twenty-five thousand dollars to the email address below, I'll be forced to sell them to the highest bidder. Pictures of this quality can sell for quite a lot, and since I've recently lost my job, my hands are tied. I've added the pictures here as an attachment so you can see they are indeed of you. Once someone else purchases these photos, they will be the owner of the content and will be free to distribute them in a wide variety of ways such as postcards, mugs, T-shirts, and blankets. Trust me, you do not want that. Send the money today and put this entire nightmare behind you. Why risk humiliation and entrapment? You have twenty-four hours. Yours coolly, a friend."

Jasper groans. "All right." He takes the phone from me. "We've got a cyber division down at the station that I work in conjunction with, but considering the nature of those photos, I think I'll have to handle this one on my own."

Clyde mewls, *I think Jasper likes the pictures.*

I shake my head over at the orange ball of fluff. "Believe me, Jasper won't look at the pictures."

Jasper blows out a breath. "Unfortunately, I'm going to have to open them all up if I want to dig into the digital stamps embedded in them. They could point me in the right direction."

Now it's Mom who's groaning. "Great. Just what I wanted. My son-in-law seeing my good side." *And to think I shaved myself silly for this nonsense.*

Georgie and Juni chuckle up a storm.

"Look at the bright side"—Georgie steps in close—"if you don't pay up, and someone makes up some merch, we could buy up the inventory and sell it right here in the shop. Mugs, pillows, blankets. We could advertise at the biker bar out in Edison. I bet we'd sell out like sweet cheeks." She winks. "Get it? *Sweet cheeks?*" She gives my mother a swat on her bottom.

"I get it." Mom is quick to shove her off. "Jasper, you have to help me. I have twenty-four hours, you saw that yourself."

"Can I use your computer?" He nods to the desk next to the register. "And I'll need to get into those emails you were exchanging with Romero." *Lord knows which will be worse to look at, the nudes or the emails.* He winces my way. *Sorry, Bizzy.*

I shrug up at him because he's right.

A sickly moan comes from my mother. *Good grief. How can I show anyone those steamy email exchanges, let alone my son-in-law?*

Fish yowls as she heads my way and I scoop her up. *This is going to be damaging, isn't it?*

Sherlock barks. *Yup—to Jasper's psyche.*

"Okay, fine." Mom tosses her hands in the air and nearly sends Clyde flying. "But you have to promise me not to read them." She navigates us over to her laptop, and no sooner does she open it up than both Hux and Macy speed their way over.

"What the hell is going on?" Hux bellows as he and Macy appear next to me.

"The fun's about to start," Juni says as she elbows Georgie. "I'll go get the folding chairs from the back."

"Good thinking," Georgie says. "And I've got a batch of those green cookies back there that I swiped from the café this morning. Bring those, too. We'll need something to munch on."

"Green cookies?" Mom balks. "I think I'm going to be green." *Hey? If I lose my lunch on the keyboard, maybe this laptop will blow up and so will the internet?*

She opens her laptop and a picture flashes over the entirety of the screen with far too much flesh and far too many curves.

An entire chorus of screams goes off, and Clyde bolts from my mother's arms, stepping on her keyboard and inadvertently launching an entire montage of horrifying pictures of my mother.

Tasteful, my foot—and how I wish it was only my mother's foot we were seeing.

"All right," Jasper shouts, holding up a hand in my brother's direction. "You're clearly too close to the situation for this. I'll look at the pictures myself."

"What?" Huxley thunders as he gives Jasper a firm shove.

Macy gasps as she scoops up Clyde. "They're going to fight! No offense to Jasper, but my money's on Hux. He might just kill somebody today."

Fish mewls, **Sorry, Bizzy, but I'm siding with Macy. It's Huxley's mother, after all.**

True.

Georgie claps up a storm. "Isn't this great, Preppy?" She's quick to goad my mother. "You've finally got two men fighting over your naked body. It's as if all of your fantasies are coming true today."

Mom glowers over at her gray-haired business partner. "You know what else I fantasize about? Wrapping my hands around your neck."

"All right," I shout. "Nobody kills anyone." I quickly fill Hux and Macy in on the threat my mother received.

"Knew it," Hux growls as he rolls up his sleeves. "All right, Jasper. We're going in and we're going to nail that bastard to a wall. Romero or whatever his name is—he's going to do some prison time over this."

"What?" Mom squawks. "No, no, no! Romero is innocent in all this. I spoke with him this morning and he said his computer must have been hacked. He says it's a common but unfortunate occurrence."

"He's not wrong." Jasper gives her an affable yet short-lived smile, the same one he uses when he's trying to defuse a situation. "All we need to do is speak to him ourselves. I have a few questions to ask him that might lead to the true perpetrator, and since time is of the essence, I suggest you give him a call right now."

Mom's mouth opens and closes. "I can't just call him out of the blue."

"You just said you spoke to him this morning," Macy is quick to point out.

"I did, on the internet. We converse through emails and text messages. Besides, I don't even have his phone number."

Jasper fiddles with her phone. "And I'm calling him." He holds up the phone and puts it on speaker.

"What?" Mom sounds terrified by the prospect. "But I don't even have his number."

"You've been texting him," Jasper points out. "You may not have realized it, but you definitely have his number."

Two solid rings drift by.

"Wait a minute." Mom looks panicked as her fingers drum over her throat. "He's in France. They're six hours ahead of us."

Hux nods. "And that means it's eight at night. I highly doubt he's in bed yet."

It rings two more times and Mom gives an exasperated sigh.

"Of course, he's not picking up," she says. "He probably doesn't recognize the number."

But before we can offer a rebuttal, the phone stops ringing as someone picks up.

"Hello?" the curt voice of what sounds like an older woman answers.

"Yes." Jasper pulls the phone close. "May I please speak to Romero?"

The line goes dead and nobody breathes.

"There you go." Mom shoots Jasper a look as if it were all his fault. "You probably called the wrong number."

"I'm sorry, Mom," Macy says as both Jasper and Hux head back to the laptop. "But you're being catfished. That woman? That was probably Romero. And I'm guessing she's mighty miffed she's not getting her twenty-five grand."

"Oh, I'm paying," Mom says it with such conviction it's frightening. "There's no way I want my face or any other part of me out there for the world to see. I'll just chalk it up to an expensive life lesson. Those are my pictures, and I want the rights back."

"You tell 'em, Toots," Georgie shouts while noshing on one of Emmie's pistachio pudding cookies. "Nobody puts your derrière on a T-shirt but me. Don't you worry, sister. I'll make sure our line of your nudie pics is nothing but top quality. And we'll charge a premium for them, too. People appreciate art more when there's a hefty price tag attached."

Sherlock barks my way. *You should do it, too, Bizzy.*

"No way," I say to both the pooch and Georgie.

You should, Clyde insists. *Sherlock always has the best ideas*, she mewls as she jumps down and begins rubbing her face against his leg. *And maybe you could sell them in the gift shop at the inn?*

Gift shop?

Fish mewls up at me, *Oh, why didn't we think of that, Bizzy?*

"I'm not selling nude pictures of myself to boost sales at the inn," I say a touch too loud and everyone in here looks my way.

Jasper sheds a devilish grin. *If you change your mind, I'll be happy to play the part of photographer.*

Hux shakes his head at my mother. "Way to be an example for your daughters."

Mom balks, "I never wanted them to see those naughty shots, let alone emulate them. Besides, I got the idea from Macy. There was no way I could think of this on my own."

My sister tries to bury a giggle fit with her hand. "Mom walked into Lather and Light last month while I was having a rather lively exchange with one of those men you were investigating." She gives me the side-eye. "Speaking of which, I'd better text James back." She takes off toward the corner and starts tapping away into her phone.

Hux and Jasper settle in behind my mother's laptop,

moaning and groaning as they pilfer through her emails and crass photos. Something tells me I'll need to figure out a way to disinfect Jasper's mind afterwards.

"All right, Biz." Georgie slings her arm over my shoulders. "Where to? I can't sit here all day looking at nudie pictures of your mother. I've already seen 'em all. She would have done better by adding a little banana pudding to the mix, if you ask me."

I nod. "In the least used a few well-placed cookies." I think about the case for a minute. "Devan and James are both prime suspects, but I'm not ruling Hadley out yet either," I whisper so Jasper won't hear.

"Don't let her off the hook, Biz," Georgie growls. "I read chapter fifteen twice and that woman has a diabolical mind."

I make a face. "I'm never finishing that book." Okay, fine. I read a few more chapters since I've last closed it. She's a good writer, but I can't get over how many times Lady Haddie had to get down and dirty with my husband. "Hey, wait a minute. Devan mentioned something the other day about Liv being upset the night of the murder. And I distinctly remember her having a tense conversation with Patterson the night he died. I say we pay Liv a little visit."

"I know just where she is." Georgie gives a wink.

"I know where she is, too. She told me herself she works down at the library," I say. "How do *you* know where she is?"

"I've had a few granny gigs at the library this week." She

makes a face. "If the demand keeps up, I'm going to have to triple my fees."

"What are you charging?" I ask and Fish meows in my arms.

If I know Georgie, she's asking for bacon.

Sherlock barks. *I want to work with Georgie!*

And I'm going wherever Sherlock goes. Clyde doesn't waste any time glomming on to her favorite four-footed friend.

She shoots the three of them a look. "I charge in donuts. Don't knock it, Biz. One day you'll be old and broke and you'll wonder where your next donut is coming from, too."

"Lovely," I say. "I guess we're off to the library. And maybe we'll get your cholesterol checked out on the way back."

Sherlock barks once again. *I'm going with you and we're not coming back unless we've got donuts.*

Georgie gives him a quick scratch. "We're on the same wavelength, kiddo. And the best part? They sell donuts now with bacon."

Georgie may not be able to read minds, but she always seems to be in tune with the animals.

Both Georgie and Sherlock howl in unison, and Clyde joins in on the fun.

Don't worry, Bizzy. Fish looks my way. *They can focus on stuffing their faces. We'll focus on tracking down the killer. I have a feeling we're getting close, Bizzy.*

"I think so, too," I whisper.

Whoever killed Patterson Higgins had better soak in the last moments of their freedom.

They won't be free for long.

CHAPTER 12

The Cider Cove Public Library sits nestled between the distal edge of Main Street and where the first tract of homes begins.

This veritable warehouse filled with portals to another world is set in a widespread wooded area. The building is a knife-sharp rectangle with tall windows filled with artwork from the local elementary school. The entire library has a modern flair to it, but try as it might to give off a cold feel, it's most certainly homey with the pine trees snuggled up against it and the cheery burnt orange hue of its walls both inside and out. The library is built against a steep slope, and the back has a porch that enables you to look down and see all of Cider Cove at a glance. It's an expansive view that I always make a point to enjoy when I'm here. But by the looks of things, I don't think I'll be heading inside today.

An entire section of the parking lot has been marked off, and there's a huge tent to the right laden with chairs and plenty of people filling them, and according to the banner strewn across the tent, we're just in time for children's—

"Story time!" Georgie shouts as she jumps around and ends up getting tangled up in Sherlock's leash in the process.

Oh goodness, Clyde mewls as both she and Fish poke their heads out of the kitty carrier. True to Georgie's word, she quickly had her quilting minions whip me up a wonky carrier in sweet floral prints of every pastel shade, and I couldn't love it or its contents more if I tried. **Should Sherlock be twisting his body that way?**

Fish gurgles out what sounds like a laugh. ***Only if he knows what side his bacon bit donuts are buttered on.***

"And if he doesn't want Georgie's footprints all over his back," I add.

A warm breeze blows past us and I turn my face toward the library, only to see rows and rows of tables set out, laden down with boxes. People are swarming the area, and a piece of cardboard with the words *used book sale* lets me know exactly what they're here for.

A woman with long silver hair catches my attention, and I quickly tap Georgie on the arm.

"There she is," I say with a touch too much excitement. I can't help it, I'm secretly hoping Liv will be the key that unlocks the door to the killer. "Come on, let's go."

Georgie gasps as she looks that way. "It's the day I wait for every month!"

Clyde spikes up so far and fast she practically leaps out of my pouch. *Free bacon day?*

"Dirt cheap books, sister." Georgie cinches her tote bag over her shoulder. "And don't worry your furry little heads. I'm getting one for each of you today, too. A book on mice for Fish, a book on salted meat for Sherlock Bones, and a book on how to land a handsome hairy dog and get him to do your bidding for you, little girl." She traipses over and scoops Clyde out of my wonky pack. "Come on, kid, you're coming with me." She takes off with Sherlock wagging his tail alongside her.

Don't worry, Bizzy, Fish mewls. *We don't need them. Let's go straight for the attack before the perp spots us and decides to run. Just let me know if you need me to claw at her while you call for backup. We're a team, you know.*

A tiny laugh bubbles in my chest. "A rather violent one it sounds like."

I snake my way through the sea of tables, and on the way I can't help but get distracted by all of the yummy, delicious, ultra-cheap books. And have I mentioned they cost next to nothing?

"Oh, Fish, look," I say, pulling a tattered paperback out of a box. *"The Secret of the Old Clock*! I just love Nancy Drew. I must have read all of her books one summer. They're what got me hooked on mysteries. And would you look at the price? That can't be right. They only want a quarter for it."

A quarter? Maybe it's missing a digit in the front.

"One would think. Why would the library give these away for free? And, oh my word—" I stop short as I scoop up a handful of pastel covered books. "Why, they've practically got the entire Sweet Valley High collection! You probably won't believe this, but I spent every Friday night and all weekend reading these books growing up. Emmie, Mackenzie, and I used to pass them around like literary candy—they were just that good. Scoot over, would you? Make some room in there," I say, stuffing as many gently, and some not so gently, used paperbacks into the carrier with her just as a box to my right filled with hardbacks catches my eye. "A dollar?" I muse at the price boldly written on the side.

Back away, Bizzy, Fish scolds. ***I know that look in your eye, and you're hungry enough to scoop up every last one of these books. Think of the cottage. There's hardly any room now that Jasper and his beast have taken up residence. You really should think about becoming a two resident home. And before you frown at me, it was Macy who suggested it the last time she visited. She was just being practical. And oh*—**she moans as I stuff a smaller Christmas themed hardback next to her—*Bizzy. Now stop that. You know that there's no place to put these.*

"I'll always find a place for books."

I know you will. I've seen them eating up the shelves in that speck of a closet of yours.

"And don't forget in those upper cabinets in the kitchen. I can hide anything up there and Jasper will be none the wiser."

That's because all he does in the kitchen is wait for you to make him a sandwich.

"Fish." I laugh. "You're awful. I love to make Jasper sandwiches. It's our thing."

Really? And how about washing his dishes? And his clothes? Are those your thing, too? Because you've doubled your chores since they've moved in, and you can't argue with me on that because I've seen it.

"True. But Jasper leaves early for work and comes home late. And he's got a commute going both ways. But don't you worry. He's grateful." And he loves to show me just about every night how grateful he is.

Well, I do know he cares for you deeply. I'm glad about that. And I know Sherlock cares for you deeply. And well, he doesn't even seem to notice me these days. It's Clyde this, Clyde that.

"Fish Baker Wilder." I press a kiss to the top of her head. "You are so adorably jealous. Don't you worry. No one can ever take your place in Sherlock's heart. And Clyde, well, she's completely gaga in love with the big lug, but could you blame her? Jasper is right. He's sort of a chick magnet." A book with a cover of a mouse on it catches my eye. "Look at this"—I'm quick to show Fish—"*Of Mice and Misfortune*," I read. "A cozy mystery caper. I'll get it for us to read by the fire." I squeeze the book into the wonky quilt carrier and it nearly ejects Fish by proxy.

A couple of regency romances catch my eye and I pick one up. The redhead beauty on the cover suddenly looks as if she's morphing into Hadley, and that dark-haired Lord looks an awful lot like Jasper from the back.

I can't help but make a face at the cover.

"Not your cup of tea, I take it?" a friendly voice chirps and I turn to see Liv Womack grinning at me while holding out a plastic tote bag my way. "And your books are about to knock your cat right out of that backpack. You might want to use this instead."

I laugh as I take the bag from her. "Thank you," I say, quickly taking the books out of my carrier, much to Fish's relief.

Leave the one with the mouse in here for me, Fish mewls. **I rather like the company.**

I do as I'm told and quickly smile back at the woman before me.

Liv's wild gray hair looks like strands made from the finest silver as it shines in the sun, and her skin looks bronzed, leaving her teeth glowing back at me.

"No to the regency books?" she muses.

"I'm just starting out in the genre," I tell her. "Actually, someone I know wrote a regency romance and used my husband as her muse."

"Ah." She tips her head back. "Hadley. So you went to the Writing Wenches meet-up? Hadley's been penning that book for a while now. She talks about it now and again—she told the group the male lead was inspired by one of her exes." She takes a deep breath and shakes her head. "She's sort of the honorary nutjob of the group. Sorry if she's your friend. I don't mean to insult her."

A small laugh bubbles from me. "No worries. And I guess I can't really blame her, I happen to be a little nutty about my husband, too."

"*Your husband* being the operative words." She gives a curt nod. **I should know.** "Believe me, I know how you feel. I had a nutter obsessed with my husband, too, once. And, well, let's just say she's his new wife and I'm the ex." **And I still hope a plane falls on their house.**

The smile glides right off my face. "I'm so sorry." I'd probably be wishing the same thing if I were in her shoes.

Fish yowls, **We won't let Jasper leave you, Bizzy. I take back everything I've ever said about the oaf. He's your oaf and you're keeping him.**

I give the tiny kitty a quick pat.

"I'm glad you have such a fun job," I say, glancing out at the sea of tables and spot Georgie with two brimming tote bags apiece on each arm. "Wow, you must really move the books with this sale."

She glances over at Georgie and laughs. "We do. All the money goes to the library fund, and it's an excellent way for our patrons to pick up some great reads on the cheap." *I won't bore her with my theory on book buying being a bona fide addiction. I know for a fact people get a natural high off it.* "And the kicker? About ninety percent of the purchases get donated right back to the library, so we get to sell them again and make more money."

"Really? That's wonderful, but it's kind of funny, too. I've donated books before but not many. I have a hard time parting with them. Once I read them, they become like friends."

"I'm the same way." *The only friends I ever want.* "But you would be surprised. Even the diehards like us are succumbing to the e-reader. It is kind of nice to have your entire library in your purse with you, so I can see the lure. Most people are pairing down their book collections to just a few these days. That's the thing about books. They do take up some serious real estate in the house. And most prolific readers are choosing to go digital."

"I get that. I certainly do both. How about that book club you're in, the Grim Readers? Do they have a preference?"

"You can read any way you like in the club," she says, straightening a few books in one of the boxes I just pilfered through. "I've done it both ways. Most people choose digital."

"Oh? At the last meeting everyone seemed to be holding a paperback."

Her lips pucker. "That's because those were distributed by the publisher. The paperbacks for that book weren't available widely, and Higgins House had yet to upload the e-book." She looks a little miffed by this.

"I didn't realize that. But now that I think of it, Devan, your group leader, came by a week before the event and dropped off a dozen copies in the event someone from the inn wanted to read it. It never occurred to me the paperbacks would be tough to find. It was a good book, though."

"Really? You thought so?"

"Oh yeah, I'm big on mystery. I mean, it was easy for me to figure out who the killer was early on, but let's just say I have a knack for that sort of thing."

She ticks her head to the side. "I'm glad you enjoyed it. You wouldn't happen to know who offed Patterson, would you? Cops came around and questioned all the members it looks like. Rumor has it, he was poisoned."

"No, I have no clue who could have killed the poor man. Did you know him?"

She glances to the sky. "From the club. He was a polarizing individual. He came to the Grim Readers as a publisher, and most members were put off by the fact he kept shoving his own books down our throats."

"I guess he wanted to promote his authors by getting some word of mouth going."

"That's exactly what he wanted. But unless a book is a real head turner, word of mouth doesn't amount to much. The truth is, he was giving out promotional copies, because technically it fulfilled his duty as a publisher to advertise the books. That's what people signed up for when they chose his publishing house. Anyway, he's dead and gone and I guess so is that publishing house, so the Grim Readers can get back to their regularly scheduled reading." She shrugs. "Everyone knows it was Devan who offed him. Or at least that's what the whispers are in the club. She's the bitter ex." She says *bitter ex* in air quotes.

"You don't believe the rumors, I take it?"

"Hard to, I guess. She's been nothing but uplifting to everyone. It's hard to picture her going dark on the sly. I guess you never know what anyone is capable of, isn't that right?"

"What about James Foreman? I heard he had a crush on Hadley—Patterson was into Hadley. And I thought I heard something about James wanting to buy the publishing company."

"James?" Her lips turn down as she expresses her amusement. "That's a new one. I mean, about the publishing house. The thing with Hadley?" She rolls her eyes. "James was always siphoning off Patterson's leftovers, so that doesn't surprise anyone. Patterson Higgins was a good-looking guy. Not a lot upstairs." ***He was as dubious as he was attractive, but I'll leave that out for now. No reason to berate the guy any more than everyone else has.*** "Anyway, Hadley wasn't really trying to seduce Patterson as far as I can tell. She was just desperate to get her book published. And I guess she couldn't meet Patterson's terms, so that's when I noticed she turned up the heat. And believe me, I think Patterson was up for some down and dirty negotiations. Hadley's a looker. Plus, she had that whole quasi-fame thing going for herself. Who knows? Maybe she offed the guy because she couldn't stand what he was leading her to do? There was a lot going on in Patterson's life that led to chaos." **Damn fool is what he was. But he thought he had all the answers. Sadly, those answers didn't work out for him, did they?**

"Well, someone killed him," I point out. "And like you said, I guess we don't know what anyone is capable of."

"Poisonous mushrooms." She shakes her head. "I suspect the sheriff's department will connect all the dots sooner than later. I mean, Devan does own the mushroom farm. I'm surprised they haven't raided her compound by now, but then, the wheels of justice are slow moving. They'll arrest her sooner or later." She smiles over at me. "Are you coming to the next Grim Readers book club? Meets Friday right here at seven-thirty."

"I'll be there. In fact, a few of my friends will be coming, too. We're already enjoying the book." I steady my gaze over hers as if willing her to give up something, anything new.

She tips her head back and squints. "You know, if I didn't know better, I'd say the killer would probably be at our next meeting, too. I've read enough mysteries to know they like to go on like nothing happened. I don't think whoever did this skipped town."

"You think they're sitting back and laughing at the fact they got away with murder?"

"I wouldn't say laughing." She cocks a brow at the thought. "But certainly they feel some level of satisfaction."

"I bet you're right." My phone bleats, and as soon as I pull it out, Liv takes off with a wave.

It's a text from Camila Ryder, of all people. I click into my phone and see it's a picture she's sent—of Hadley and Jasper locked in an embrace.

It's going down right now in his office, Bizzy. Get down here fast and put on a show for me.

I grab Georgie, toss a fifty-dollar bill at the woman working the register, and we take off for Seaview. If I owe more to the library, I'll ante up later.

Right now I have a regency rake to fry.

CHAPTER 13

The Seaview Sheriff's Department is muggy and stifling inside.

"Here's hoping the AC is broken and it's not Hadley and Jasper bringing all the steam to the building," I say as Georgie and I race with our furry friends over to his office and we come upon his secretary extraordinaire, Camila herself.

"*Ooh*, goody." She wiggles her shoulders. "The fun can begin. Go—storm in there. It's your God-given right. Make a big stink about it, too. I would never have tolerated Jasper to two-time me."

Camila doesn't have to tell me twice. I barrel through the door, only to find Jasper at his desk, Hadley seated across from him, and a pizza nestled between them.

"Bizzy?" Jasper's eyes bug out a moment.

But before I can say a single thing, toss a shoe, or a *pizza*, Georgie arches her back, thrusts her head back, and belts out a wild howl that seems to be summoning all the beasts in the great state of Maine. Fish hops out of my arms, as does Clyde. I didn't have time to fuss with the wonky carrier, and the two of them hop right onto Hadley's chest and begin to yowl and make a great show of swiping their claws. Sherlock starts in on a barking spree that only rivals Georgie's howls—and from behind Camila is chronicling it all on her phone.

"Enough," Jasper thunders as he jumps to his feet. "Bizzy, I swear this is not what it looks like," he says, attempting to pluck Clyde from off of Hadley and I do the same with Fish—although Fish is putting up a good fight, and I think she's successfully unraveled a part of Hadley's cantaloupe-colored cardigan.

"I'm sorry," I say to the woman. "About your sweater," I add just to be clear. "You'd better stay away from my husband."

Hadley laughs while Georgie and Camila come up on either side of me.

"I'm afraid you caught us catching up and nothing more. I'm no homewrecker." *Yet.* "My apologies to you all." She bats her lashes over at the Duke of Homicide. "Thank you for the pleasant conversation." She forces a smile my way as she hits the exit. *If she keeps up this lunatic act, he'll be mine sooner than later.*

I blow out a breath because I'm half-moved to agree with her.

Jasper has me in his arms before I can blink.

"I would never do a thing to hurt you. I swear, she stormed in here fifteen minutes ago with a pizza and it's been untouched ever since. And to be honest, I was just about to get rid of her."

Georgie clucks her tongue. "That's what they all say." She strides over to the pizza box and flips it open to reveal a fully intact cheesy-looking pie. "So I stand corrected. You didn't lie about the pizza."

"I didn't lie about anything," Jasper says it with a sober tone.

Sherlock belts out a few more barks. *You tell 'em, Jasper. I knew you aren't a cad, whatever that means. I knew you would never hurt Bizzy in any way.*

Fish hisses, *It wasn't Jasper we were worried about. It was that cheap hussy. I'm betting we stormed in just in time before she took all her clothes off.*

Clyde mewls, *How shameful that would have been. It's embarrassing enough the poor people only have a tuft of fur on their heads.*

Fish's ear twitches as she looks to Clyde. *It's not shame-*

ful. And did you know our kind could be hairless as well? I hear it's quite fashionable these days to have a hairless in the household. A guest at the inn had one not long ago, and let me tell you, he was a looker.

Ooh, a looker? Clyde purrs so loud even Sherlock lifts an ear her way.

"I believe you," I say to Jasper. "I apologize for storming the castle. It's just—Camila sent me this picture of—"

Georgie steps in "Of you and Hadley locked in an embrace." She wags a finger at him. "That's some hard evidence. We came with receipts, as the kids say these days."

"Bizzy—" Jasper starts and I shake my head.

"I have no doubt she lunged at you," I tell him. "And I don't think there's anything wrong with you embracing whoever you like. I guess seeing it unleashed the jealous genie from the bottle. Forgive me?"

"Do you forgive *me*?" he insists and both Georgie and Sherlock coo in unison.

"Please," Camila gags. "Bizzy, that woman is out to snag your man. Today she comes bearing pizza, but next time it'll be her with a bow wrapped around her waist. I know her type. She's going to watch the two of you like a hawk, just hoping for a crack in the armor, and then she'll pounce when he's vulnerable."

I glance back at her. "So does that mean she'll be taking a page out of your playbook?"

She sheds a greedy grin as she strides past me. "You

know me well." She snatches up the pizza and walks right out of the room.

"I gotta run, kids." Georgie hitches her head that way. "I'm splitting that pizza with the she-devil. And once I'm through, I'll be distributing my card to the men in blue. You'd be surprised how many hunky men still need a grandma in their lives. Just yesterday I got paid overtime to iron a pair of slacks and whip up a batch of chocolate chip cookies."

"Georgie." I wrinkle my nose. "Be careful. There are freaks out there."

"Don't worry about me. I charge more than a few freaky dollars."

"What's you're flat rate?" Jasper asks.

"Give me five hundred smackers, and I'll do your bidding for the day."

"Sold," he says. "How about you drive Bizzy's car back to Cider Cove? I've got somewhere I'd like to take her."

"I take cash or credit," she says, scooping up Fish and Clyde. "I'll see you kids later. And Jasper? Try to squeeze a cake into that mystery date. Nothing says *I'll never leave you for another woman* than a slice of triple chocolate fudge cake."

"Will do," he says, and Georgie, the cats, and Sherlock sail on out the door.

"Ooh, a mystery date?" I muse. "*And* cake? We're not going to a bakery, are we?" I tease, but secretly I'm sort of rooting for the bakery.

"I'll gladly take you wherever you want right after I make all of our mushroom dreams come true."

I take in a breath. "You got the warrant?"

"Yup. Just landed on my desk twenty minutes ago. Are you in, Detective Wilder?"

"I'm in."

And just like that, we're out of there.

❖❖

BRAMBLE POINT IS LESS than a half hour drive from Seaview, and we arrive at Abner Farms just an hour before it closes to the public.

It's country out here, nothing but farms for miles, and a cheery red sign reads *Welcome to Abner Farms* as we drive under its arches. Of course, we're not alone. A few patrol cars are following along, filled with people from toxicology ready to take some soil and water samples. Jasper told me that he let Devan know the other day that they would be coming in force, but that it was strictly procedural seeing how the victim died. He also told me that he didn't get too far with tracking down whoever is terrorizing my mother. But he did convince her not to send a single dime. Here's hoping it worked.

We park, get out, and Devan comes out of a large two-story structure to greet us.

Nearby are three smaller structures that look like modern barns comprised mostly of dark slats of wood. The acreage stretches out before us in every direction. To the right there are a few cows and a horse penned up in a corral, and to the left there looks to be an ample vegetable garden with lots of green leafy goodies and a few tomato plants as well.

"Welcome," Devan greets us with a wide smile, and behind her are a handful of women. She's dressed in a red flannel, jeans, and cowboy boots, looking perfectly homey and charming. "Your deputies are free to go wherever they like. I'd just appreciate it if they didn't trash the place. My co-owners will show them around." She motions behind her, and the men and women here from forensics head that way. "But as for you two—" Her brows furrow a moment as she tries to make sense of me. "Bizzy?"

"That's me." I shrug. "This is my husband. Once he mentioned he was coming to your farm, I had to tag along. I've never been to a mushroom farm before."

"Well, come on. I'll show you around." She navigates us into the first building behind her, and it's wide and brightly lit with closed doors to the right and left. "We keep all of our mushrooms in contained environments, and every species of mushroom has its very own grow room. And that's precisely what happens there—they grow. We've got an extensive system throughout each of the four grow centers, and each one is meticulously monitored for light and climate control. Some of the species require a bit more babying than others, sort of like men." She winks my way and a laugh bubbles from me. "Let's head in this one." She opens the door for us, and Jasper and I are led into a cavernous room that's dimly lit, cool, and slightly damp as the scent of fresh soil bites our nostrils. Rows of pods laden with mushrooms line the walls. These in particular are orange with wavy bottoms that look like miniature frilly skirts, and it looks as if we've just been transported to some exotic forest.

"Stunning," I say.

"Aren't they?" She shakes her head as she looks around with a satisfied smile. "They're my babies. These are chanterelles. I'll make sure to send you home with some. Just sauté them in a pan with a little butter and serve with your favorite meal."

"The first three buildings is where the action happens, and in the last building we do the packaging and sorting."

"How did you get into this?" Jasper asks as he runs his finger over one of the delicate blooms.

"I was having a hard time after my divorce, and I knew I wanted to go into business for myself. A few of my girlfriends were feeling the same, and we took our time until we found something we could get passionate about—and something that was needed in the area. It turns out, the mushroom business is booming. And not only that, but restaurants love to boast of farm-to-table vegetables, so we thought we'd start here. We applied for an agricultural loan and got a little seed money. We scampered for the rest." **No thanks to Patterson for holding out on me.** "And regardless of our obstacles, we now have a thriving business."

"You're a real go-getter," I say, still marveling at the elongated elegant necks of this curious looking mushroom.

"You know if I ran into this in the woods, I don't even think I'd realize it was a mushroom."

"Chanterelles are highly coveted by chefs. They have an airy, fruity flavor, and once you have them, you'll never want to go back. I take a little home with me just about every night. Now, if you did come upon this in the wild, I wouldn't pick it. The chanterelles have a twin called the jack-o'-lantern mushroom and he's poisonous. Not the same mushroom that killed Patterson, but it could do the job. In fact, the rule of thumb is, if you didn't buy it from a farmer or the grocery store, don't eat it."

"Thanks for letting me know." I take a moment to examine her, and she looks so open and honest. She doesn't have a single nerve twitching, despite the fact she's having her business presently searched by the authorities.

Jasper ducks to look into one of the racks where the pods are sitting. "So if someone were to grow poisonous mushrooms at home, how easy would that be?"

"Are you kidding? If you have a front lawn, you already know the answer. It doesn't take much. No one loves a lawn full of mushrooms, but everyone loves it here. A few months back, we had the Grim Readers here on a day trip, and afterwards I served everyone a big lunch—lots of homegrown veggies and mushrooms—and then we had our club meeting."

Jasper and I exchange a glance.

That could have been the birth of an idea, he says, and I nod his way because I completely agree.

"Devan"—I lean in—"where would someone get their hands on a death cap?"

She pulls her cheek to the side as she considers this. "Whoever did this must have done at least your rudimentary Google search. They're prevalent across Europe and we have some in North America as well. They're all over California, and here in Maine you can find them attached to pine trees, but our weather is so harsh in the winter it's hard for them to thrive. Now, there are people who sell stuff like this. So if someone is determined, they could have purchased them."

I sigh at the thought. "I guess the world is your oyster if you're set to commit something nefarious."

She nods as she looks to Jasper. "Did you talk to James Foreman?"

"Yes"—Jasper winces—"but I can't give any information on how that went."

"You don't have to." A laugh rises in her throat. "I know exactly what he's up to. I heard he's making a bid for Higgins House. And I just can't see that happening. And it won't. Besides, his heart's not in it. Before Patterson passed away, I spoke to James and he said he was thinking of moving to New York and getting into finance with his brother. He said he couldn't live off of what he was making and something needed to change. I guess things didn't work out with the brother." Her phone chirps and she glances at it. "I'm needed in the next building over. Please feel free to poke around here." She pulls a bag off the counter and a knife. "Go ahead and fill it to the brim. It's on me. And don't forget, next book club this Friday night at the library—seven-thirty. Come for the coffee if nothing else." She takes off with a wave and the door closes quietly behind her.

"What do you think?" Jasper asks, waving the knife in his hand her way. "Or more to the point—what did *she* think?"

I shake my head. "She didn't have a single errant thought. And she's sticking to her guns. She thinks James did this. And he did have wine in his hand that night—wine he says he didn't imbibe."

"Okay, we'll keep trucking. In the meantime, let's fill up this bag and check the rest of the place out. I believe we have a bakery to get to."

We do just that. We fill that bag until it's brimming and walk around the different buildings on the grounds. Jasper and I wouldn't know a death cap if we were holding it in a bag, so we take off, pick up a cake before we hit the cottage, and have a party for two.

Jasper lets me know I'm the only woman he has eyes for, one kiss at a time.

And a delicious time is had by all.

CHAPTER 14

The next afternoon there's enough sunshine to power a nuclear reactor, and I'm not complaining. I've always felt as if I come alive under the warmth of its healing rays, and trust me when I say, there is nothing better than being out on the cove under an umbrella while reading a good book—or even a really, really bad one.

"Ugh." I groan as I slap closed the cover of *The Duke and*

the Lady. "The woman is relentless," I tell Emmie who's sunbathing on the next lounger over. We've both donned our teeniest bikinis and we're relaxing just a few feet from shore under the girth of a thatched umbrella, each with a cold, fruity drink by our side. "Not a scene goes by without her getting down to business with my husband."

"Why are you doing this to yourself?" she asks without so much as taking her eyes off her copy—which was technically Georgie's copy, but once Georgie finished it, she lent it to Macy, who lent it to Mackenzie, before it finally made its way to my bestie.

"I don't know," I growl as I watch the waves lap the shore.

The cove is filled with tourists today, and there are colorful umbrellas staked as far as the eye can see up and down the sand. The scent of burgers and hot dogs on the grill mingles with the salty brine, and summer is well on its way. Kids are chasing one another, mothers are chasing after their kids with suntan lotion in their hands, boogie boards abound in the water, and there is an entire army of people lying on beach towels—and wonky beach quilts as we soak in the first yummy rays of the season. Yes, Mom and Georgie's quilting endeavor has taken the cove by storm today, and I'm glad about it, too. Not only are their wonky quilts adding a cozy touch to the beach, but it makes me happy to see their business thriving.

Fish, Clyde, Sherlock, and Emmie's labradoodle Cinnamon are lounging under the umbrella along with us, playing with the toys Emmie and I brought for them. Well,

Fish, Sherlock, and Cinnamon are playing with the toys. Clyde is sprawled out over Sherlock's back once again. It seems to be her favorite place to take a nap, and don't think for a minute Fish hasn't been irritated to no end about it. I've never seen her so worked up. She can't think Clyde is going to swoop in and steal Sherlock's affection for her. She's just being irrational.

"What do you think of the book?" I can't help but ask Emmie as she continues to bury her nose in it. "I mean, you must like it. You're turning the pages so fast, you're creating a breeze."

"*Bizzy.*" A laugh bellows from her, and I won't lie, I find her joy just a tad bit annoying. "I'm loving it. But only because I'm picturing Leo and me as the main characters. If I think of Hadley and Jasper in those roles, I'd want to vomit. And judging by that expression on your face, that's exactly what you want to do right now. Do yourself a favor, and don't read the book."

"Ha," I grumble. "And not find out what happens after that cliffhanger on page fifty-two?"

"You're only on page fifty-two? Bizzy, you might want to put that book down. The heat level only goes up from there. Let's just say, I'm taking mental notes for my wedding night. I might really wow Leo with some of these moves."

I openly growl right at her. "Okay, fine. I'll stop reading. What's happening with your wedding? The ceremony is all set to take place right here at the gazebo, and then the reception on the beach right after. What about your dress? What about my dress? Let's talk food."

She bubbles with a laugh. "Don't worry about the menu, and the cake—I'm taking care of all of it. The kitchen is handling it. And yes, Leo and I insist on paying for the food. You're already sacrificing by not charging for the use of the gazebo and the reception venue. I know for a fact you lost out on paying bookings because of me. As for my dress, I'm thinking about wearing my mother's dress, or just pulling something out of my closet."

I gasp without meaning to. "Oh, Emmie."

"No, it's okay. My mother's dress is an eighties monstrosity. I gasp when I see it in person each time myself. But I'm in talks with a seamstress who thinks she can get it close to my dream dress."

"Aw! The sweetheart neckline with full lace sleeves and bodice?"

"That's the one. I feel like we've sketched it out on paper so many times, I'm surprised we haven't conjured it by now."

We share a warm laugh.

"Don't worry," I tell her. "You're going to get your dream dress. And your dream wedding, too. I'm going to do everything in my power to make sure that happens. Just like I'm going to make sure Hadley doesn't get her dream wedding to my husband."

Emmie laughs alone this time. "Your paranoia is amusing. But I can assure you, my wedding will be the only one Jasper will be taking part in this summer."

It's true. Jasper is the best man and I'm the maid of honor.

Bizzy? Clyde whips her furry little orange tail over Sherlock's back. *What's a wedding? Do cats get one, too?*

Cinnamon barks. *Of course, cat, dogs, and any animal can have one. It's when two creatures fall in love and want to tell everyone around that there's no one else for them. What's his is hers, and what's hers is his. I'm married to Gatsby. He hates the sand in his fur or he'd be here right now.*

Gatsby is Leo's golden retriever, and Cinnamon is right. He's not a fan of the hot sand, or the hot sun. He likes to come out in the evenings and run through the shoreline during the cool of the day.

Clyde mewls my way, *I want a wedding, too, Bizzy! I want to marry Sherlock Bones, and that way no other creature could have him.*

Sherlock barks. *That's a great idea. That way you could give me backrubs all the time and we don't have to worry about angry poodles trying to chase you away.*

What? Fish screeches. *And what about me? What about all the backrubs I've given you these past few years? What about curling up at night with me? Why am I suddenly feeling like yesterday's chew toy?*

An odd vocalizing sound comes from Sherlock. *Don't worry, Fish. You're still my girl. In fact, I'll have two wives. What do you think of that, Bizzy?*

"Exactly what I'm afraid Jasper will say to me next." I quickly relay the conversation to Emmie and she belts out a hearty laugh.

"It's funny to you," I sniff. "Back to your wedding. You're getting married in June. That's just two months away." I suck in a quick breath. "That means next month I have to host a shower."

"You don't have to host anything. Actually, I prefer if you didn't. My mother has been threatening, too, and I've already shut her down over it."

"I'm calling your mother, and we're having it here at the inn. We'll do high tea with little petit fours, macarons for dessert, and a lush cake, of course, along with lots of pastel balloons. You'd better get online and start creating an inventory so we can navigate the guests in the right direction. I'll have to send the invites out in a week if I want to pull this off."

"Bizzy, don't you dare. What am I going to do with a service for twelve fine china?"

"You're right. We'll ask for twenty-four. That way if you have an extra guest or break a few you're covered."

She bubbles with a laugh "No, thank you. Have you met me? I'm more of a bring-your-own-food-and-meet-me-at-the-grill kind of a girl. Besides, both Leo and I are already having a hard time consolidating so we can fit into my cottage."

"Aw! I'm so glad you're staying on the grounds. We're going to do couple things all the time. We should plan a vacation together."

"You won't have to," a familiar voice says from behind. "You live at a resort."

I turn around to see my mother holding a folding chair

while wearing a see-through cover-up over her skirted one-piece bathing suit. My mother has always been modest at the beach for as far back as I can remember. Macy used to tease our mother about her mid-thigh-length swim dresses by calling them our mother's beach formals.

Georgie is right there with her with a folding chair of her own, but she's chosen to remain sheathed in one of her famed kaftans, a light blue number today.

We exchange polite greetings as my mother and Georgie get settled next to us. And no sooner do they sit down than Jordy stakes another umbrella in the sand for them.

"Hey, Bizzy." Jordy's lips twitch, but he doesn't flash one of his signature smiles my way. He's got sunglasses on, but I don't need to see his eyes to know he's still pretty down about being a suspect in Patterson Higgins' murder investigation. "Any break in the case?"

"Not really. But I wouldn't worry. You're so far down the suspect list, the only thing killer about you is your looks."

"Funny." He attempts a smile, but it never initiates. "I just can't wait to have this behind me. And I can't wait to see who the real killer is. I'm emotionally invested in getting them behind bars. I feel as if they targeted me that night to take the blame. I bet they'd love for me to serve their time, too."

Emmy laughs at her brother. "Don't worry, Jordy. You won't have a single excuse to miss my wedding."

"I'm not missing that bachelor party either." He mock shoots her before taking off back toward the inn.

"Speaking of painting the town with banana hammocks"—Georgie starts and Emmie is already groaning—"don't think we're going to miss out on throwing you the wildest Irish wake you've ever seen."

"Irish wake?" Mom balks. "Georgie, that's akin to a funeral. I'd ease up on those magical brownies you're eating. You mean *bachelorette* party."

"I've been married, Preppy, and so have you," Georgie says. "I mean wake. But don't worry, Emmie. The first two or three years aren't that bad. It's when he finds a young twenty-something named Tina that it really starts to stink."

"Sometimes her name is Juni," Mom muses while slathering herself with coconut-scented suntan lotion.

It's true. Juni replaced my mother as my father's new bride at some point, but I think she was farther down the matrimonial line.

"And life gets expensive once you get married, too." Georgie lifts a brow toward my mother. "And apparently, being single costs a fat roll of nickels, too. Tell 'em what you did, Prep."

"Georgie," Mom hisses while swatting her over her armrest with the book in her hand—a copy of *The Duke and the Lady*. "You promised you wouldn't say anything."

"I'm not saying anything." Georgie swats back before scooping up Fish. "I'm letting you do the honors."

All four pets are suddenly rapt at attention for whatever is about to transpire.

"Okay, fine." Mom tosses her hands in the air and Fish bounces in her lap. "I negotiated with the person who was threatening me, and I got them down to a decent price."

"You got them down to a decent what?" I shout so loud half the cove looks this way momentarily.

"You know they wanted twenty-five grand," she continues. "And I got all the pictures back for a cool two thousand. That's a twenty-three thousand dollar negotiation."

"You negotiated with terrorists?" I balk. "What does Huxley have to say about this?"

I won't even ask about Macy. For all I know it was her idea.

"Hux doesn't know, and he's not going to know. Bizzy, those pictures were humiliating. All that Hux and Jasper were able to do was try to track the pictures and the emails electronically. They admitted it could take weeks if they discover anything at all."

"Mom." I close my eyes an inordinate amount of time. "Please promise me you will never do that again. And while you're at it, please don't engage in any more text messages with that Romero person—who as evidenced by yesterday's phone call is a *woman*."

"Oh, he is not a woman. It was all a mix-up. His aunt picked up the phone while he was in the shower and she doesn't speak good English. Besides, I won't have to text him for too much longer. He's coming here to Maine."

Emmie and I exchange a look.

"Go on." Georgie motions for her to continue. "Get to

the good part, Preppy. The part where you had to send him a couple grand as well."

I inhale so sharply I'm positive my lungs are full of sand.

"Do not tell me that," I grit the words through my teeth.

"Fine." Mom relaxes back in her seat while giving Fish a hearty massage. "I won't tell you that. He needed a few dollars to make the trip back to the States. Not that it's anybody's business what I do with my hard-earned money."

"It'll be my business once you're bankrupt and living with me," I grouse.

"Don't you put that curse on me," Mom teases.

"I won't have to. That invisible man you're dating will do it for me," I say. "When is he supposed to touch down on U.S. soil? I for one cannot wait to meet him."

"Saturday."

Emmie and I exchange another far more alarmed glance.

She shrugs my way. "I guess this is really happening."

"Maybe," I say, but I'm not all that convinced. "But first we need to get through one more book club meeting with the Grim Readers." Tomorrow night.

And hopefully we'll all have a killer good time—with the killer I'm about to apprehend, of course.

CHAPTER 15

*E*vening came, Jasper brought home a pizza for us —he said we couldn't let Hadley ruin one of our favorite meals, and I agreed so much that there's none left for a midnight snack. Evidently, I was out to prove a point.

The sea breeze came in cooler than expected so we built a fire. Sherlock is sitting in front of it watching as Fish teaches Clyde all about the ways of the world—

starting with a little thing called monogamy. Too bad Lady *Haddie* couldn't be here for the lesson herself.

Jasper comes back from the kitchen and lands next to me on the sofa with a plate full of the pistachio pudding cookies I brought home from the café.

"How's it going?" He nods to my phone.

I've spent the last ten minutes in a group text with Hux and Macy telling them all about our mother's latest not-greatest misadventures with love and money.

"Hux is threatening to meet Romero at the airport with a shotgun. And Macy is wondering if he has a cute hot son."

"Sounds about right."

Macy texts again. **And great news! I'm writing a book!**

"A book?" Jasper and I say in unison.

Stop right there. Hux texts. **I can only deal with one insane relative at a time.**

Macy texts back. **Very funny. Bizzy. Can you get it started for me? You know, like you used to with my papers when I was in school?**

Jasper groans. "Please say no. Macy is old enough to do her own homework."

"You're so right." I quickly text back. **Macy, I am not writing your book for you.**

My phone lights up again as she sends another message my way. **Jasper told you to say that, didn't he?**

A laugh bursts from me. **I can speak for myself. The answer is still no. What are you writing a book for, anyway? You hardly like to read.**

LOCK, STOCK, AND FERAL

She texts right back. **True, but I have a publisher already waiting for me to meet my deadline. James says he might acquire Higgins House and that I could be his official first client.**

"A publisher?" Jasper snaps up another cookie. "Things just got interesting."

Huxley fires off another text. **What are you going to write about? The time your mother got swindled out of house and home?**

Macy texts back. **House and home are the same thing. Sheesh, and you're supposed to be the smart one? Enough about Mom, back to me. James said he'd wave all the fees and take care of all of my publishing needs.**

"Shows what she knows," I say. **Publishers don't charge fees.** I hit send.

The dancing ellipses light up my screen until Macy pops up again. **I don't know what fees are involved. Production costs, things like that.**

Hux is up next. **That house and home thing is an expression, Macy. Speaking of which, I need to leave the office. I have a hungry, cranky wife I need to tend to. And don't either of you dare say I said that. I'll talk to you both Saturday regarding the big catfishing reveal.**

"Ooh, we should get together," I say, quickly typing into my phone. **Late lunch at the cove? Say two-ish? The café has a stellar menu now that we've revamped it.**

Hux texts back. **See you there. I'll be gunning for the lobster.**

Macy hits send again. **I meant it about that book,**

Bizzy. We'll brainstorm on Saturday. Get some good sleep the night before. I'll need you sharp as a tack to come up with some bestseller list worthy ideas. Think steamy romance. And no dead bodies!

"There's that," I say, holding up my phone to Jasper. "Saturday is going to be filled with family, seafood—"

"And maybe a shotgun."

A laugh rumbles from me. "That's why you and Leo both need to be there with your weapons at the ready. Maybe wear a Kevlar vest. I'd like for you to come home in one piece."

A thought hits me and I reach over and pick up his laptop.

"I wonder if the website for Higgins House mentions anything of his passing," I say, opening it up and running my fingers over the keyboard in an effort to get us there.

Fish mewls and jumps up onto the couch next to me and Clyde comes over on the other side of her.

Maybe there's a condolence page, Fish yodels. *I bet the killer has already left his or her mark.*

I translate for Jasper and his chest bumps with a silent laugh.

"The killer certainly left his mark," Jasper says. "But you're right, Fish. Killers usually like to come around again if they can. They like to hide out in the open. It makes them feel better than hiding out under the covers."

Or running away. Sherlock barks. *Why don't any of these killers ever hop on a plane and head for warmer climates?*

I glance his way. "Because if they did, we'd never catch them."

"We'd catch them." Jasper lands a kiss to my cheek. "You're just that good."

I purr like a kitten as I snuggle up against him. "Here it is, Higgins House Publishing," I read as we take in the orange background with silver script writing scrawled across it.

Higgins House Publishing? Clyde chirps. *I heard someone mention it the night of the murder—before I was captured by your sister, Bizzy. It sounded like two men.*

I relay it to Jasper.

"Go on," Jasper says, picking up the tiny kitten. "Do you remember what they were talking about?"

One of them said, 'You'll make me a partner. With the two of us at the helm, we might actually make a profit for everyone.'

I quickly fill Jasper in. "What else did they say, Clyde?"

Then the other man said, 'You'll be in business with me over my dead body. No offense, but I'm making enough money without you.'

Jasper's chest expands. "Sounds like Patterson and James were going at it."

"Sure does," I say, clicking the *about* section of the Higgins House website. "Higgins House"—I say as I start to read the tagline off the page—"where all of your publishing dreams can come true. For inquiries, send a writing sample via email and we'll let you know if your book is a good fit for our company." We scroll through the website and read over the extensive list of clientele and peruse their books on the website as well.

"Everything seems so normal," I say. "Business as usual. But then again, I suppose that's business."

"Agree," Jasper says. "Let's try inputting Patterson's name in the search engine. There might be an online bereavement journal we can find. Usually the mortuary provides one for the family."

"Let's see." We type in his name, but nary a commemorative journal of any kind pops up. Instead, Patterson Higgins' name is found on a few website forums for writers.

"Huh. Let's check that out," I say, clicking into the first article at the top of the page, which leads us to a website called The Writer's Nest.

"There he is." Jasper points to Patterson Higgins' name under a thread called *help me find a publisher for my manuscript*. "Higgins House takes just about anything. Just be prepared to fork out the big bucks. They're a bit on the pricey side, but they claim to do a lot of handholding," he reads.

"Wait a minute." I pull back to get a better look at my handsome hubby. "Publishers don't charge authors. I think this is kind of what Macy was talking about."

Jasper clicks to the next page. "Look at this response." He points down to the next comment. "They're not quality and they certainly didn't hold my hand. But they sure did hold out their *hand* when I forked over twelve grand."

"Oh no," I moan as I look up at Jasper. "Do you think Patterson Higgins was a vanity publisher?"

"Someone who charges a mint to produce the work and then pockets the proceeds?" His cheeks twitch. "It's not ethical as far as publishing houses go."

"I know. I had a friend in college who got mixed up in one. She thought it was a legitimate publishing house that wanted to take on her work, and it turned out they took on any book they came upon—for a fee, of course. Her book never sold more than a few copies, and that was just to friends and family. She ended up with an entire garage full of boxes of her books. She went on to do great things in the book world, all within traditional avenues, but Higgins House sounds like the exact place she warned everyone to stay away from."

"Wow." He hands me a cookie. "I guess we know why James said that with his help they could make a profit for everyone."

"Hey"— I say, pulling the cookie close—"James said something to me to the effect that Patterson had over six hundred angry authors."

"That's a lot of people to add to the suspect list. Okay, so we know James may have wanted Patterson out of the way in an effort to lay claim to the publishing house himself and to sink his hooks into Hadley. Let's review the other five hundred and ninety-nine suspects."

I make a face. "There's Hadley herself. She had some insane desire to publish that triple X fantasy she wrote about you. In fact, I remember her thinking that night that she was about to secure a contract with him—and that it had something to do with her body." I rack my brain to try to recall every last detail. "And then I remember her saying she had no part in Patterson's demise, and her next thought—she confessed to having a part in it."

Jasper casts a glance to the ground. "It's hard for me to believe that Hadley could be capable of something like this, but when people are passionate about something, they're capable of anything."

"And then there's Liv Womack. I saw her having a tense conversation with Patterson that night, too. She had wine, they all did—even the one who claimed he didn't. I'm not sure what that tense conversation was about, but I did read her thoughts and she did say that Patterson was a damn fool who thought he had all the answers."

Jasper grunts, "I don't know that I'd disagree with her there, especially knowing what we do know regarding that vanity press he was running."

"Agree. And then there's Devan, mushroom farmer extraordinaire. She was his ex-wife, too."

Sherlock barks. *Doesn't that mean what's his is hers, and hers is his?*

Clyde mewls, *It does if they were married. That's what Cinnamon said this afternoon.*

"That's right." I look to Jasper. "Wait a minute—I think Devan mentioned she was still married to Patterson when he acquired the publishing company from his uncle."

Jasper leans back, his eyes locked to mine. "That means, unless he bought her out, she'd have a vested interest in it."

"And it just might revert to her upon his passing. Jasper, you have to come to the book club tomorrow night at the library. I can try to pick her brain and see if she confesses to wanting the press."

"I'll do you one better. I'll start digging into it as soon as I hit my desk in the morning. It might take cutting through some red tape, but I think I have some friends in legal who can help me trace the underpinnings of Higgins House. If we can figure out the year it was acquired, the year of their divorce, and whether or not he did anything to legally remove her, we could have another solid motive."

"And the woman knows her way around a mushroom. There was plenty of room on that farm to grow just about anything."

Clyde mewls, *I can't see a wife wanting to poison her husband.* She hops off the sofa and makes her way over to Sherlock before snuggling up to him.

I can, Fish yowls.

Come on, you. Sherlock gives a soft bark and pats his paw on the other side of him.

Oh, fine, Fish growls as she slinks down and curls up on his other side.

"Sherlock is playing both sides of the fence," I whisper.

"Rest assured, I am not." He lands a kiss to the nape of my neck just as his phone goes off. He plucks it off the table and examines the screen.

It's a text from Hadley. **Just thinking about how kind you've been to me. Thank you for understanding. I wish I were strong enough to tell you about our child all**

those years ago. I hope you'll find it in your heart to forgive me. Goodnight.

I look up at Jasper and he shakes his head at me as he puts down his phone.

We wrap our arms around one another and hold on tight.

And my heart breaks for both of them.

CHAPTER 16

The Cider Falls Public Library shimmers like a star in the sea of never ending darkness as Georgie, Juni, my mother, and I make our way into the building. Of course, I came equipped with Fish and Clyde in my wonky pet carrier strapped to my chest. And once Sherlock Bones heard where we were going, he certainly didn't want to miss out on the fun, so Georgie said he could tag along for the adventure, posing as her emotional support animal.

"Who needs emotional support at the library?" Mom frowns over at Georgie. "And you're no better, Bizzy. You don't see me hauling around Mistletoe and Holly everywhere I go. Okay, sure, so I've taken them here or there, but never to a library."

Georgie scoffs. "And that's exactly why they can't read."

"I'm not here for the reading." Juni adjusts her hot pink vinyl skirt that cuts off just below her hips. I'm terrified of what's going to happen should she sit down. "I'm here for the hunky male librarians."

"They have those here?" Mom cranes her neck toward the crowd before us, suddenly interested in tonight's outing for more testosterone-based reasons.

The library is brimming with both books and bodies, chairs have been set out near the palatial area that sits between the new releases and the reception counter, and there's a refreshment table near the patio doors with coffee and water set out on it. Not nearly the ritzy spread we had the night Patterson was killed, with the cheese and the wine. I bet the library has a no alcohol policy. Or maybe I'm the only goof they've ever found who was willing to accommodate them. Not that I pitched for the liquor. And in the rear, the back patio doors are opened to that spacious deck that overlooks all of Cider Cove, and I can't wait to go out there and check out the view once we're through in here.

Fish mewls as she warms my chest, **Here comes Macy. I didn't know she wore glasses.**

"Neither did I." A laugh bounces from me as Macy steps up clad in black with red-framed specks that take up half her face. "Hey, four eyes," I tease.

She makes a face as she steals Clyde from me. "You laugh it up, but now that I'm an author, I need to look the part."

"An author?" Mom gasps with pride like only a mother can. "Macy, that's fantastic. What in the world are you writing about?"

Georgie swats her. "Don't you know? She's put together all of her after-hours escapades into one steamy compilation, and now she's ready to take the book world by storm. Publishing today—a three-part movie deal tomorrow."

Juni sighs. "And we get to say we knew her when."

Macy chokes. "A steamy compilation? Why didn't you think of that, Bizzy?" she asks, shoving Clyde back my way. "I'd better go jot that down. I brought a notebook tonight in the event you had a brainstorm or two I could steal. Who knew it was Georgie's brain I'd be after?"

"Stick with me, kid," Georgie says, linking arms with Macy and handing Sherlock's leash over to me. "I've got ideas for a sequel that will knock your socks off."

They disappear into the crowd just as Juni inhales a sharp intake of air.

"All right, Ree"—Juni straightens— "hottie naughty librarian of the male persuasion over by the paperback racks. Try not to make that annoying wheezing sound when you breathe. If you're nice, I'll see if he has a brother for you."

"A brother, for *me*?" Mom flattens her skirt with her hands. "Stand back and watch a pro. I'm about to land that man for myself—for fun, of course. I've got a real man coming in tomorrow."

They take off as if a box of donuts were in the bounds. And I bet by the end of the night, they'd rather have a box of donuts.

A soft meow bleats from Clyde. ***Now why would Ree want to get in the way of Juni landing that hottie naughty? She's got the man she sent the nudie pics to.***

Fish yowls, ***Because Ree****, much like some other creatures* —she pauses to shoot Sherlock a dark look—***likes the chase of it all. Love is real, Clyde, but on occasion, people simply like the affection they garner from others.***

Sherlock offers a muffled bark. *I like the affection, I confess.*

"Let's hope I can get the killer to confess tonight as well," I whisper.

"Bizzy?" a chipper female voice chimes from behind, and I turn to find Liv Womack with her silver hair lying over her shoulders like a white waterfall. She's donned a khaki dress and manages to look just as scholarly as Macy. "How I love that you brought your pets." She gives all three of my furry friends a quick scratch. "Usually unless they're seeing eye dogs, pets are a no-no in the library. But women are forever coming in with purse puppies, and we just look the other way—just like I'm going to do for you tonight."

"I appreciate that. I can stay out on the patio if it's a problem."

"No way. It's chilly out and dark. Besides, all the action will be in here. You won't be able to hear a thing out there. Go grab a cup of coffee and settle in. You're going to love it. This is one of the favorite places for the Grim Readers to meet. We've had other outings before, too—the beach at midnight, a haunted house, all the sensational things Devan can think of." She averts her eyes, and a little laugh bounces from me.

"Well, it was fun having you all at the inn." I cringe as soon as the words leave my lips. "I'm sorry. I meant up until things took a deadly turn."

"Oh, that's okay. It was fun being at the inn up until that point." *And a little after that, but that's just me being morbid. Speaking of morbid...* "Here comes Devan." She nods past me. "I heard her arguing with James earlier. Something about Higgins House Publishing." Her lips tug to the side. "I think it all ties back to Devan's farm. She said so herself that she's over her head with expenses. I heard her telling Patterson just a few weeks back that she was on the brink of destruction if he didn't give her what he owed her."

My mouth falls open. He *owed* her?

"If you don't mind, I think I'll go make sure everyone is getting settled. I plan on staying out of her warpath tonight." She takes off, and I turn just as Devan is about to pass me by.

"Bizzy." An instant smile comes to her face as she takes in my menagerie. "Oh, give me this sweet little kitten." She plucks Clyde out of my front pack. "And hello to you, sunshine." She gives Fish a tickle. "And you, too, handsome." She blows a kiss to Sherlock before setting Clyde back in my arms.

For a killer, she sure is insightful. Sherlock gives a soft bark back.

"I think that was a thank you," I tell her and she laughs.

"I miss having pets. And I really need a cat, or a small army of them. I wasn't kidding when I said I could use one at the farm. We've got a terrible problem with mice." She rubs her nose to Clyde's. "And I bet you, little miss, would be an ace at chasing them, too."

I would! I really would! Clyde is quick to mewl right back.

Devan gives a full-bellied laugh.

And to think this might just be the killer—the most jovial killer I've met to date.

I'm about to make light of Clyde's enthusiasm when Hadley Culpepper steps into the room with a tight black lace dress on cut down to there and riding up to here, and all heads turn in her direction as she boldly strides our way.

Devan's chest pumps with a dry laugh. *Well, if it isn't Little Ms. Slut. Patterson sure took pleasure rubbing her in my face that last night we were together. What the heck is she all dolled up for? This is a book club, not prom night. Unless, of course, there's some other poor shmuck she's here to land. I can't stand to watch.*

"Excuse me, Bizzy." Devan forces a smile. "I need to

prepare for the meeting." She jets off just as Hadley steps my way, glancing to my left and my right—looking for my poor schmuck of a husband no doubt.

"Evening." She sighs with defeat as she comes up empty. "So where's Jasper?"

"Oh, he'll be here. He's just running a little late."

Fish pats me on the chest. *You shouldn't have told her that.*

Clyde meows. *She's looking to snare him for herself, Bizzy.*

"That's wonderful." Hadley pulls her shoulders back and her boobs nearly fall out of her dress. "I mean, that's wonderful that the two of you do things as a couple." *Not that you'll be doing them together for long. I've been told I'm irresistible in this dress, and I plan on testing out that theory on my Duke tonight.*

A choking sound emits from me. "How dare you."

"How dare I what?" *Don't tell me Sherlock Homely here has figured out my connection to Patterson's death.*

I suck in a rather dramatic lungful of air. "You killed him, didn't you?"

"What?" She takes a step back and examines me, head to foot, as if seeing me for the very first time.

"You said you played a part in his demise, I heard you." Albeit in my mind, but if she's going to play dirty with my marriage, then I'm playing dirty, too.

"Did I say that?" Her fingers fly to her lips as she looks momentarily stunned. *I would never have said that out loud. Oh, this is bad. This is going to make me look guilty. Jasper will think I'm a killer. Worse yet, he'll lock me up behind bars for doing the deed.*

"Did you do it?" I take a breathless step forward. "Did you kill him that night?"

"What? No! The part I played in his demise had to do with his *business*. I was talking to people at the Writing Wenches about the fact that Higgins House was charging an astronomical fee to publish my book. Word got around that Higgins House was a vanity press—and well, I inadvertently tarnished his reputation. But I was still going to use his services. Higgins House was simply a vehicle to get my book to market. Once the world read *The Duke and the Lady*, they would have fallen in love with us."

Her bosom quivers as if she were starring in a regency romance right this minute. But too bad for Hadley because she is not getting a happily ever after with my husband.

"Okay, fine. Maybe you didn't kill him." I crane my neck past her at the blooming crowd.

Where to now, Bizzy? Fish yowls.

Let me claw at her face. Clyde gives a sharp meow. ***That'll teach her for thinking she can steal your man. You're married to Jasper, for goodness' sake. What doesn't she understand?***

"Exactly," I say under my breath.

"Exactly what?" Hadley shakes her head at me with a newfound aggression. "You just wait until Jasper hears that you've spoken to me so tersely, and after accusing me of murder no less." ***That man will be mine before the night is*** *through, and I didn't even need to stuff my feet into these heels to get him.*

She stomps off before I can stop her—not that I would have.

I turn around and spot James headed in this direction wearing the same knitted sweater he had on the night of the murder, and a book tucked under his arm, giving him a rather adorable bookworm appeal.

"Bizzy, how are you doing? Is Macy here?"

"That depends if you mean Racy Macy or Macy the Author. The studious version is running around with a pair of red glasses on. So, I hear you're looking to publish her nonexistent book." I frown up at him. "People have done a lot of things to get in my sister's pants, but never a book deal. That's a first."

Easy. Sherlock barks. *He could still be the killer, Bizzy. He had that glass of wine, remember?*

Clyde mewls, *The wine he said he couldn't drink because he's a diabetic, or was it diuretic? I've heard Juni talking about the latter. Maybe that was it?*

She had it right the first time.

"James"—I say his name a little harsher than I meant to, considering I'm still rattled from my meet and greet with Hadley—"can I ask you a question?"

If Hadley isn't the killer, and Liv isn't the killer, that just leaves Devan and James. I think it's best to eliminate James right now. At least then I can let Jasper know we're on the right track.

"Yes." His brows grow close. "Anything, what is it?"

"The other night at the club, you mentioned you were diabetic and that you couldn't have wine—yet I saw you in line for wine that night Patterson was killed. And then I saw you with it later in your hand."

He inches back, his brows furrowed. "Bizzy, I don't know what you're implying"—he takes a moment to chuckle—"but you're right. I was in line that night to get wine, and I did get some. I saw a gorgeous woman in the room, and I wanted to offer it to her." *It's a tried-and-true tactic to get lucky, but I'm not about to share that with the woman. After all, it's her sister I eventually got lucky with.*

A hard groan comes from me. "I'm sorry." I grimace. "But I'm glad to hear you weren't sneaking a sip of something that could hurt you."

"Not a problem. I know we're all on edge." He gives the back of his head a scratch as he looks into the crowd. "Holy hot glasses," he practically drools as he says the words. "I'll catch up with you later, Bizzy," he says as he bolts in my sister's direction.

It was Macy he had gotten the wine for, Fish grouses. *I don't know why I didn't think of that.*

"Me either," I say.

Devan is about to zip past me when she offers Sherlock a quick pat.

"It's almost showtime," she says, looking my way. "Help yourself to some coffee if you need it. It's strong. "

"Oh, I could use something stronger," I tease. Especially now that I'm certain she's the killer.

"Sorry." She straightens. "No wine tonight. That was

sort of a one-off. In fact, we've never had wine at one of these functions. I don't like to attract people just because they think there's an open bar. We're not that kind of book club."

Clyde mewls, *I bet she needed the wine to disguise the taste of that poisonous mushroom she tainted Patterson's drink with.*

I nod at the tiny kitten.

"So what made you choose to have wine that night?" I ask a little too smugly because I already know the answer.

"Oh, I didn't want it. But Patterson said the author insisted. I guess she was there that night. He never did have the chance to introduce us." She glances to the crowd. "Ten minutes until we begin," she chirps. "I'm always a little too excited at these meetings." She takes off, and I can hardly catch my breath.

"The author requested the wine," I pant.

The author was there? Fish meows.

Who was the author? Sherlock barks. *What do they look like?*

"I don't know. I can't remember the author's name." I pull out my phone and look up the book online—*Lock, Stock, and Double Barrel Peril.*

The book pops up and so does a picture of the author. S.L. Teller is staring back at me. And just like that, I know who the killer is.

CHAPTER 17

Bodies swirl around me as I navigate my way through the crowd. The din of voices rises ever so slightly as the library eschews one of its most golden rules tonight, that of silence.

I won't be silent either once I corner my very next suspect. And if things go the way I think they will, this will be my very last suspect of the night.

Text Jasper. Sherlock barks. *I won't let you do this, Bizzy. I promised Jasper that I wouldn't let you walk straight into danger. And this person is dangerous, they've already killed once.*

Clyde lets out a roar. *Let me at 'em. I've been anxious to give chase and catch a mouse, but a killer will do in a pinch.*

Fish looks up at me. *That explains all the chasing that's been going on back at the cottage. Clyde has far too much energy to be pent up there. Perhaps instead of hunting down the killer on our own, we can try to find her a new fur-ever home?*

I shoot a look down at my wily but sweet cat. "Nice try, but I'm going to talk to that woman. I have to know if I'm right."

What about Jasper? Sherlock all but pulls me backward by way of the leash.

My phone bleats, and it's a text from Jasper himself. "I won't have to text him."

I wave the phone at Sherlock. "He says he's on his way."

Without further ado, I spot my mark as she steps out onto the patio and I'm right on her tail.

It's dark out, the air is crisp, and my ears clot up with the silence as the chatter behind me begins to dissipate. There's nary a soul around as I make my way over to the far end of the patio and step right next to the suspected killer as we take in the glittering view of our cozy town.

"It's magnificent, isn't it?" I say, taking in a lungful of fresh spring air perfumed with honeysuckle.

"Oh, Bizzy"—she jumps back as her hair glows like a

white flame in the night—"you about gave me a heart attack." She clutches at her chest and laughs before giving Sherlock a quick pat, but he backs up a notch and gives a light growl in response. "Easy, boy," she teases. "That's okay. I'm not offended. I suppose everyone looks a bit menacing out in the dark. We should get back inside."

"Yes," I say, stopping in front of her. "But we have a few minutes. Would you mind if I asked you a question?"

"Anything. I've worked here for thirty years. I know every nook and cranny of this place. But if it's not library related, I probably don't know diddly."

"I'm guessing you do," I say as my breathing picks up the pace.

Liv Womack's eyes glow right along with her hair under the light of the third quarter moon.

"You know a lot about books, I don't doubt that," I tell her. "And I think you know a little about how they're written, too. Isn't that right?"

Sherlock whispers, **And here we go again.**

Fish hisses, **Keep it down. Bizzy knows what she's doing. But in case things get out of hand, be ready to attack.**

"I'm sorry?" Liv leans in as if she couldn't have heard me right.

"Patterson Higgins ran a publishing house. Higgins House," I say. "James called the authors poor shmucks. Would you agree with that?"

Boy, would I ever. She chuckles to herself. "I suppose if James said so. He would know." **He was probably ripping us off himself.**

"You know because you were one of those authors, weren't you?"

She inches back a notch. *So she's pegged me as an author. So what?*

"I—I guess the cat's out of the bag." She goes to pet Fish and Clyde, and both cats sink a little lower in the carrier they're sitting in. "I was part of the Writing Wenches—along with Hadley." *Maybe if I remind her of the woman who was trying to steal her man she'll leave me alone. I'm afraid once the book club begins, I'll have to leave Cider Cove. I don't have the blood pressure to deal with this kind of questioning. I should have left town ages ago.* "Isn't that Hadley in there now with the low-cut dress?" She clucks her tongue as she looks into the library. "And that handsome detective is with her, I think." *I don't see either of them, but that's neither here nor there.*

"I heard that wine was never served at one of these events before—not until the night Patterson died." I give a short-lived smile.

Oh good. She's changed the subject. For a moment I thought I was caught red-handed.

Liv's chest fills with her next breath. "Yes, well, we like to mix things up, I suppose."

I shake my head. "I heard the author requested it." I take a breath. "The day after the murder you visited the inn. When I asked where I could find Hadley, you said she was a writer, that you've talked shop with her before. That's because you're a writer, too, aren't you? S.L. Teller. That's you, isn't it, Liv?"

She gasps as she takes a step back and her face dissolves into the night shadows.

"No," she whispers.

"Yes," I counter. "You mentioned you were divorced and wished you had changed your name that same day you visited me at the inn. Your maiden name was Teller, wasn't it? And the day of the murder, Patterson called you Shelly. Shelly is the S in your nom de plume and L must stand for Liv."

A horrible groaning noise comes from her before she takes a breath. "And so you've pegged me. You've uncovered my alias. What now? I suppose you'd like an autograph? If you'll excuse me, I'll go get a book to give you." She tries to step around me, but I'm right there blocking her path once again.

"That won't be necessary. I'm not here for an autograph. I'd much prefer a confession."

"A what?" Her voice is sharp and echoes into the expanse behind me.

"You heard me," I growl. "The day after Patterson was killed you came to the inn and told me that you went out west a few weeks back to visit family. And I bet you brought back a little toxic souvenir, didn't you? You said you went to So Cal—Southern California. That's where you went, isn't it?"

"A vacation? That's what has you up in arms?" *I'm truly paranoid because everything she says has me jumping. I have to get away from this woman—from this state.*

"Death caps grow rampant in California," I say, trying

to temper my breathing. "And that's exactly how you killed Patterson Higgins. You boiled those mushrooms down and created a toxin so powerful it stopped his heart after a few sips of that wine. You needed the wine to mask the taste. Which I'm guessing you gleefully handed him a glass of. It was a perfect way to kill Patterson, and to set it up to make it look as if his ex-wife was the culprit. She is the reason you decided to use a poisonous mushroom, isn't she?" Her mouth opens a notch, but not a sound comes out. "He was your publisher, Liv, but he cost you a lot of money, didn't he? The day we spoke you mentioned you blew through your retirement. He's the reason for that, isn't he?"

Her head tips up as she glowers at me. "Yes, I did kill him, Bizzy." Her voice is suddenly calm and smooth.

Fish growls, **Let's leave. We have the confession. Let's get out of here.**

"You don't know what it's like for a woman out there," Liv continues. "After my divorce, I was struggling. I spent all of my life dreaming that one day I would be this great author—I handed Higgins House my baby and they trampled on it and *me*. Patterson asked me to give him thirty thousand dollars. I bought the deluxe package. I cashed out my retirement. I put it all on the line because Patterson Higgins said he could take me and my book to new heights. He promised me people would be clamoring to read the words that I wrote. And it was all a lie. The only thing he ever did for his clients was feature them with the Grim Readers. No other book club would even entertain him. He must have really had to grovel with Devan to get her to agree. I was furious."

"It was the pig in the poke scam, wasn't it? Just like the one you wrote about in your book."

"Yes." A smile twitches on her lips. "But unlike the killer in my book, I'm not going to prison."

Without warning, she knocks me backward, and I land hard on my back as I teeter over the railing.

Below me there's a drop that measures fifty feet at least and I can see the glow of jagged rocks that wait for me.

Both Fish and Clyde take off with a razor-sharp yowl as they begin to claw at Liv. And I can hear Sherlock growling and gurgling as if he were biting down over her, and I have no doubt he is.

"I'm sorry, Bizzy," Liv grunts as she pushes me another few inches and I struggle to grab onto the railing and hold on for dear life. "You made me do this. I never meant to drag an innocent woman such as yourself into this."

I'd remind her about Devan, but I don't dare move a muscle.

"I'll let everyone know it was an accident," she hums the words as if she were singing a lullaby. "I'm sure Hadley will take good care of your husband."

It's as if every cell in my body were suddenly filled with adrenaline, and I launch forward, grabbing onto her head and nearly toppling us both over the edge.

"Freeze!" a masculine voice thunders, and before I know it, Liv lifts both of her hands in the air and my body begins on a free fall right up until my hand hooks onto the railing. "Bizzy!" Jasper hoists me over to safety before ducking back into the library after Liv, and I run in after them both.

Sherlock leads the way, barking up a riot, and Jasper quickly tackles Liv down in the horror section.

It seems appropriate. She's caused quite the horror.

Soon, she's cuffed and a swarm of sheriff's deputies arrive on the scene to haul her away.

"Are you hurt?" Jasper pants as he takes me in with a scrutinizing gaze that travels up and down my body at lightning speeds.

"I'm fine," I say, relaxing into his arms. "I just want to go home."

And we do just that.

CHAPTER 18

Normally, after a night like last night, I'd want to stay in bed all day with the covers pulled up over my head—especially since I have Jasper here to hunker down with. But I've invited everyone down to the cove and promised them an amazing lunch starring our new seaside-inspired menu, and that's what brings us to the beach.

"Bizzy"—Emmie moans as she swallows down one last bite of her lobster pie—"the new menu is the stuff of my dreams. Thank you for making them all come true. I've wanted to revamp that menu for years."

"The old owner wouldn't have approved, but I'm glad I did. Best decision ever," I say as Jasper, Leo, Macy, Georgie, and Juni join us out on the back patio of the Country Cottage Café. The sun is out, the skies are clear, the scent of burgers on the grill is making everyone moan with delight, and the waves look so inviting, even someone as deathly afraid of large bodies of water like myself is almost enticed to run into the sea. Almost.

I glance out at the cove and catch a glimpse of Sherlock, Cinnamon, and Gatsby running around on the sand. I'm happy Gatsby decided to brave the sand in order to have fun with his friends. And while they do that, Fish and Clyde enjoy a lazy nap, curled up together on a chair to my right. It's nice to see that Fish has finally taken to Clyde as well.

I nod back over at Emmie. "And the menu is just perfect for summer. Speaking of summer," I say as I look at Leo and Emmie, "the two of you are staring down the matrimonial barrel. I'm so excited, you'd think it were Jasper and me getting married all over again."

Emmie gasps. "Why don't you do it? The two of you should renew your vows right alongside us. You know I've always wanted to have a double wedding."

"No way," I tell her. "This is your special day. Jasper and

I will renew our vows in silence as we watch the two of you. Nothing is going to steal your spotlight."

Emmie's expression dampens on a dime. "Not even a killer?"

"Not even a killer," I'm quick to tell her.

"Come on, Bizzy." Leo smirks. "Don't make promises you can't keep."

"Watch it." Jasper crumples a napkin and tosses it his way.

Emmie reaches over and gives my hand a squeeze. "I'm just glad I'm on the right side of the law. I'd hate to have you on my tail. And Jordy says thanks for catching the killer, too. You're our hero, Bizzy. I think you deserve a cape made out of wonky quilts."

"You're hysterical."

"I'm being serious," she contests.

Georgie lets out a horrid groan, and for a moment everyone is set on edge, half-afraid she's about to regurgitate her meal.

"Are you okay, Georgie?" I ask in a panic.

Juni waves me off as she works to shell another crab leg. Both she and Georgie had the deluxe seafood tower—one apiece. It's meant to be shared by six to eight people, but the last time I pointed it out, Georgie gave me the finger—with a crab claw, of course.

"Mama's just fine," Juni snorts. "She just needs a reset before she can go in for more." She slaps her mother on the back and Georgie lets out a horrid belch.

"Took you long enough," Georgie says as she stretches

her arms to the sky as if she hadn't a care or a bellyache in the world. "Now let's see about getting some of those pistachio pudding cookies for dessert."

"I'm on it." Emmie spikes out of her seat just as Macy moans something that sounds sickly.

"What is it, Mace?" I lean her way. "Do you want me to swat you on the back as well?"

"Do it and die." My sister has never been one to mix words. Macy had the surf and turf special, along with the clam chowder bowl and the coconut shrimp and pasta combo. She's never been one to turn down a free meal either.

She moans again as she points toward the walkway, and I turn to find Huxley, Mackenzie, and my mother heading over. Huxley and Mackenzie were kind enough to head to the airport with my mother to pick up her mysterious new beau.

The entire lot of us scrambles to our feet and meets them halfway. Hux looks ready for a day at the beach, a vast difference from his usual attire of a suit and tie. Mackenzie is a diehard with those power suits. She's donned a forest green one, and speaking of the hue that nature loves so much, she looks a little green around the gills. Her stomach is starting to take shape, though, and it warms me to think that's my niece or nephew cooking in there.

Mom is in full preppy mode with a powder pink button-down blouse with the collar popped, tapered jeans, and a sourpuss on her face that can mean many things.

"Well?" Georgie cranes her neck past them. "Where's your Romeo, Toots? Is he parking the car?"

Juni nudges her. "I bet he's in the men's room. It's been a long trip for him."

Huxley crosses his arms as he looks at my mother. "Well, you want to tell her?"

"No," Mom bites back. "I'm not in the mood to talk to anyone. I don't even know why you brought me down here. I told you I wanted to be dropped off at home."

"I'll tell them," Mackenzie snips as she gives us a beady-eyed look that suggests we shook down *her* mother for money. "We got to the airport—two hours away." She takes a moment to shoot Mom the side-eye. "Only to discover that Ree wasn't exactly sure which airline he was on—nor did she know what time his plane was landing."

"He said noon!" Mom clenches her fists. "And how many airlines could there be coming from France at that time, anyway?"

"It doesn't matter." Hux relaxes his shoulders with a look of defeat. "There wasn't a Romero on any of them." He looks to Macy and me. "She doesn't even know the guy's last name. And the kicker?"

Mackenzie pulls Hux back. "She gave that shyster another five grand last night, and that's the last she heard of him."

"Oh, stop." Mom turns toward the ocean while holding herself. "I'm an old fool, and I was taken advantage of. I'm not the first one, and I won't be the last."

Georgie sags at the thought. "I'm sorry, Preppy. I'll cut

you in on my Rent-a-Grandma gig, and I'll only charge you a thirty percent finder's fee." Georgie and Juni swoop to her side, and the three of them take off in the sand a few feet away.

I'm about to go over and join them when I spot Devan Abner headed this way with a large-brimmed hat and a sundress.

Jasper takes up my hand, and we head in her direction.

"Devan," I say, surprised to see her. "You look great. Ready for a day at the beach?"

Fish, Clyde, and Sherlock run up, leaving Cinnamon and Gatsby to continue to kick up sand as they chase one another to the shoreline and back.

"I came to say thanks, Bizzy." Devan offers a mournful smile. "And thank you, Detective, for sussing out the killer among us. The Grim Readers are typically a peaceful bunch, and we want to stay that way."

"It wasn't me." Jasper wraps his arm around my waist. "It was all Bizzy."

"Thank you to you both," she says, cooing down at Fish and Clyde before scooping them up into her arms. "At least now my farm can get back to normal. Rumors started to spread after the sheriff's department turned up in droves that day to take samples. And now that I'm in the clear, my phone has been ringing off the hook all day—taking in more orders than I can handle. I guess people love an underdog." She pecks a kiss to Clyde's cheek. "How about this little cutie? If you're still looking for a home for her, she's welcome to come and live at the farm with me." She looks down at the orange sweetheart. "How would you like to be in charge of catching all the mice, kiddo?"

Can I, Bizzy? Clyde's tail whips back and forth like a pendulum.

"I guess it's a match made in mushroom heaven," I say.

Sherlock barks. *I'll come visit, kiddo.*

Fish pats Clyde over the top of her head. *And I'll be there, too.*

Devan laughs and cries and rocks Clyde as if she were her brand new baby, and for all practical purposes, she is just that.

I'm about to offer her a cold drink on the house when I spot a redheaded bombshell traipsing over in an itty-bitty bright red bikini and a pair of cherry red heels to match.

Here comes trouble, Fish murmurs, and I agree with her completely.

"Jasper!" Hadley's eyes light up as she waves and heads this way.

"Come on," I say as Jasper and I take a few steps in her direction.

Hadley lunges at Jasper and collapses over him with a firm embrace. "I didn't get a chance to thank you for your bravery." Her hands swim up and down his back, and don't think the fact she's pressing herself into him as much as possible has slipped by me. Any harder, and she's going to leave a dent.

He pulls back and looks my way *Sorry. I wanted no part in that.*

"Oh, Jasper." She curls her finger under his chin, forcing

him to look at her. "How did I ever let a man like you slip through my fingers?" *I'm not holding back anymore. Bizzy is just going to have to find another man.* "I'm glad we've reconnected. I've missed our friendship." *Among other things.* "We'll have to get together. I still have so much to tell you about the baby, the pregnancy." *And that's one lifetime bond that will hold us together. Not even his dizzy busybody wife could lay claim to him in that way. Sure, the baby was a figment of my imagination, but desperate times call for fictional babies.*

"What?" I squawk so loud, a couple of seagulls overhead squawk right back. "You lied? You lied about losing Jasper's baby? Because there was no baby!"

Hadley's mouth rounds out as she looks from me to Jasper. "I didn't say that. She must be jealous. I'm so sorry, Bizzy. But I would never make up something so heinous."

Jasper groans as he looks at her in a whole new light. "Hadley, you lied?"

Her mouth opens that much wider. "I can't believe you're just going to believe whatever she says."

"She's my wife, and unlike you, would never make something like that up," he tells her. "Why did you do it?"

She shakes her head. "No, it was true. I swear it." *What are they going to do? Ask for proof?*

"Yes." I give a wild nod. "Give us proof."

Hadley gasps as her eyes widen my way. "Well, I—"

"Leave," Jasper says it harsh like a reprimand.

"But Jasper"—she grabs ahold of him in desperation—"I saw what a mistake I had made. I never should have left. It was stupid. I thought I loved someone else for a hot second, but over the years I've come to realize it was just you who my heart belonged to. We could still have it all. We can make an entire tribe of babies. We're right for one another, you and me."

"No, we're not. You did me the biggest favor when you left that day. I may not have seen it then, but I do now. Bizzy is the one and only woman for me. Please leave."

Fish yowls at the woman, and Sherlock barks until she turns around and struts off with a huff. And both Sherlock and Fish escort her right off the property.

"Jasper." I pull my handsome husband in hard and mourn with him one more time over a child that never existed. "That was cruel. But I promise you we're going to have children one day." I pull back with tears in my eyes as I look at my sweet husband. "As many as you want—as long as it's under five."

His chest rumbles with a quiet laugh. "As long as you're by my side, I've already got all the family I need. But a couple of miniature versions of yourself would be adorable, too."

"And a couple of miniature versions of yourself would be pretty cute as well."

We share a mouthwatering kiss that says *I love you* as we assure one another the future is ours alone.

"Ree?" a husky male voice shouts from behind us, and we pull back to see a tall, muscular man with an ear-to-ear grin waving at my mother from the sand. He has a head full of black hair, comely features, a navy suit on and a bright red tie that sits slightly askew. There's something familiar about him, but I can't pinpoint just what.

"*Romero?*" my mother balks in disbelief, and soon everyone in the vicinity gasps in disbelief as well—with my brother, sister, and me leading the pack. "You're here!"

"That's right." He jogs over to her and pulls her into an embrace before spinning her in a circle.

Huxley staggers their way. "What in the hell?"

I shake my head at the sight as we watch, amazed, as my mother and her mystery man share an embrace for the ages.

Romero, the man-hungry scam artist, is not only real—he's right here in Cider Cove.

My mother pulls back and laughs as she looks to all of us gathered around them.

"See?" She points his way. "I knew he wouldn't let me down. He's almost too good to be true."

That's exactly what I was thinking.

Something tells me he's about to prove to all of us that he is, in fact, too good to be true. A shiver runs up my spine as I inspect Romero's cheesy grin.

Trouble has come to Cider Cove, and I have a feeling it's going to be a long, hot summer.

***T‍HANK **you for reading!**

Need more Cider Cove? Grab Itching for Justice (Country Cottage Mysteries 16)

My name is Bizzy Baker, and I can read minds—not every mind, not every time but most of the time and believe me when I say it's not all it's cracked up to be.

A cooking competition is taking place at the inn and a celebrity chef is set to grace us with his presence along with his fabulous food. The best part? It's the exact chef I'm hoping will cater my best friend's wedding in just a couple of weeks. Along with that the mystery man that was catphishing my mother has suddenly shown up in Cider Cove, and I don't trust him as far as I can throw his rock hard body. Speaking of bodies—I seem to have stumbled upon another corpse. But lucky for me, a perfectly adorable Samoyed works right alongside me and my sweet pets to help try to solve the case. But if we don't solve it soon, it will be a recipe for disaster.

RECIPE

**Country Cottage Café
Pistachio Pudding Delights**

Hello, it's me, Bizzy! If ever there was a comfort cookie that has that extra something, it's this one. Emmie's pistachio pudding delights are just that—delightful. And since they're green, they're a fun addition to the holidays as well. Enjoy!

Ingredients

    1 3/4 cups all-purpose flour
    ¾ cup firmly packed light brown sugar
    ½ cup granulated sugar
    1 ½ teaspoon vanilla extract
    1 egg
    1 three ounce package of pistachio instant pudding mix
    2 teaspoons baking powder

½ teaspoon salt
½ cup chopped pistachio nuts
3-4 drops of green food coloring

Directions

Preheat over to 375°. Line two baking sheet pans with parchment paper.

1. In a large bowl whip butter, brown sugar, and granulated sugar until light and fluffy, then add in vanilla and egg until well blended.
2. Add in pudding mix, flour, baking powder, and salt. Mix well until a dough-like consistency is achieved.
3. Toss in chopped pistachios and drop in food coloring, mixing well into the dough.
4. Roll dough into walnut-size balls and set on baking sheets about two inches apart.
5. Bake for 10 minutes then remove from oven and let cool.
6. *Emmie's note: These cookies are perfectly chewy and delicious. The only crunch they yield is from the nuts. But I promise they are not only delicious, they're addictive!
7. Enjoy!

A NOTE FROM THE AUTHORS

Look for **Itching for Justice (Country Cottage Mysteries 16)** coming up next!

Thank you for reading **Lock, Stock, and Feral (Country Cottage Mysteries 15).** If you enjoyed this book, please consider leaving a review at your point of purchase. Even a sentence or two makes a difference to an author. Thank you so very much in advance! Your effort is very much appreciated.

BOOKS BY ADDISON MOORE

Paranormal Women's Fiction

Hot Flash Homicides

Midlife in Glimmerspell

Wicked in Glimmerspell

Cozy Mysteries

Meow for Murder

An Awful Cat-titude

A Dreadful Meow-ment

A Claw-some Affair

A Haunted Hallow-whiskers

A Candy Cane Cat-astrophe

A Purr-fect Storm

A Fur-miliar Fatality

Country Cottage Mysteries

Kittyzen's Arrest

Dog Days of Murder

Santa Claws Calamity

Bow Wow Big House

Murder Bites

Felines and Fatalities

A Killer Tail

Cat Scratch Cleaver

Just Buried

Butchered After Bark

A Frightening Fangs-giving

A Christmas to Dismember

Sealed with a Hiss

A Winter Tail of Woe

Lock, Stock, and Feral

Itching for Justice

Raining Cats and Killers

Death Takes a Holiday

Country Cottage Boxed Set 1

Country Cottage Boxed Set 2

Country Cottage Boxed Set 3

Murder in the Mix Mysteries

Cutie Pies and Deadly Lies

Bobbing for Bodies

Pumpkin Spice Sacrifice

Gingerbread & Deadly Dread

Seven-Layer Slayer

Red Velvet Vengeance

Bloodbaths and Banana Cake

New York Cheesecake Chaos

Lethal Lemon Bars

Macaron Massacre

Wedding Cake Carnage

Donut Disaster

Toxic Apple Turnovers

Killer Cupcakes

Pumpkin Pie Parting

Yule Log Eulogy

Pancake Panic

Sugar Cookie Slaughter

Devil's Food Cake Doom

Snickerdoodle Secrets

Strawberry Shortcake Sins

Cake Pop Casualties

Flag Cake Felonies

Peach Cobbler Confessions

Poison Apple Crisp

Spooky Spice Cake Curse

Pecan Pie Predicament

Eggnog Trifle Trouble

Waffles at the Wake

Raspberry Tart Terror

Baby Bundt Cake Confusion

Chocolate Chip Cookie Conundrum

Wicked Whoopie Pies

Key Lime Pie Perjury

Red, White, and Blueberry Muffin Murder

Christmas Fudge Fatality

Murder in the Mix Boxed Sets

Murder in the Mix (Books 1-3)

Murder in the Mix (Books 4-6)

Murder in the Mix (Books 7-9)

Murder in the Mix (Books 10-12)

Murder in the Mix (Books 13-15)

Murder in the Mix (Books 16-18)

Murder in the Mix (Books 19-21)

Mystery

Little Girl Lost

Never Say Sorry

The First Wife's Secret

Romance

Just Add Mistletoe

3:AM Kisses

3:AM Kisses

Winter Kisses

Sugar Kisses

Whiskey Kisses

Rock Candy Kisses

Velvet Kisses

Wild Kisses

Country Kisses

Forbidden Kisses

Dirty Kisses

Stolen Kisses

Lucky Kisses

Tender Kisses

Revenge Kisses

Red Hot Kisses

Reckless Kisses

Hot Honey Kisses

Shameless Kisses

The Social Experiment

The Social Experiment

Bitter Exes

Chemical Attraction

3:AM Kisses, Hollow Brook

Feisty Kisses

Ex-Boyfriend Kisses

Secret Kisses

Naughty By Nature

Escape to Breakers Beach

Breakers Beach

Breakers Cove

Breakers Beach Nights

Escape to Lake Loveless

Beautiful Oblivion

Beautiful Illusions

Beautiful Elixir

Beautiful Deception

A Good Year for Heartbreak

Someone to Love

Someone to Love

Someone Like You

Someone For Me

A Totally '80s Romance Series

Melt With You (A Totally '80s Romance 1)

Tainted Love (A Totally '80s Romance 2)

Hold Me Now (A Totally '80s Romance 3)

Paranormal Romance

(Celestra Book World in Order)

Ethereal

Tremble

Burn

Wicked

Vex

Expel (Celestra Series Book 6)

Toxic Part One (Celestra Series Book 7)

Toxic Part Two (Celestra Series Book 8)

Elysian (Celestra Series Book 9)

Ephemeral Academy

Ephemeral

Evanescent

Entropy

Ethereal Knights (Celestra Knights)

Season of the Witch (A Celestra Companion)

Celestra Forever After

Celestra Forever After

The Dragon and the Rose

The Serpentine Butterfly

Crown of Ashes

Throne of Fire

All Hail the King

Roar of the Lion

ACKNOWLEDGMENTS

Thank YOU, the reader, for joining us on this adventure to Cider Cove. We hope you're enjoying the Country Cottage Mysteries as much as we are. Don't miss **Itching for Justice** coming up next. It's springtime in Cider Cove! A book club heads to the inn and so does murder. Thank you so much from the bottom of our hearts for taking this journey with us. We cannot wait to take you back to Cider Cove!

Special thank you to the following people for taking care of this book—Kaila Eileen Turingan-Ramos, Jodie Tarleton, Margaret Lapointe, Amy Barber, and Lisa Markson. And a very big shout out to Lou Harper of Cover Affairs for designing the world's best covers.

A heartfelt thank you to Paige Maroney Smith for being so amazing in every single way.

And last, but never least, thank you to Him who sits on

the throne. Worthy is the Lamb! Glory and honor and power are yours. We owe you everything, Jesus.

ABOUT THE AUTHORS

Addison Moore is a **New York Times, USA TODAY,** and **Wall Street Journal** bestselling author. Her work has been featured in **Cosmopolitan** Magazine. Previously she worked as a therapist on a locked psychiatric unit for nearly a decade. She resides on the West Coast with her husband, four wonderful children, and two dogs where she eats too much chocolate and stays up way too late. When she's not writing, she's reading. Addison's Celestra Series has been optioned for film by **20th Century Fox.**

Bellamy Bloom is a **USA TODAY** bestselling author who writes cozy mysteries filled with humor, intrigue and a touch of the supernatural. When she's not writing up a murderous storm she's snuggled by the fire with her two precious pooches, chewing down her to-be-read pile and drinking copious amounts of coffee.

Printed in Great Britain
by Amazon